40 WINKS

Stories from Slumberland

Kevin Moran

www.aninkmover.com

For the dreamers, both aspirational and asleep.

Falling Asleep

The microseconds that exist between you falling asleep and staying awake rattle your brain and make reality not so real. Your brain occupies a foggy area where clarity isn't a word. Everything before that moment is tangible and can be grasped, but going forward all things are indescribable. In this realm your senses lie, people aren't who you expect, places don't exist and all of the knowledge in the world can't help you.

Your brain scrambles to make the right connections but only gets more confused when it finds nothing but dead ends. Everything your mind tries to put together only adds to the chaos, like a math problem that gives a different answer on every attempt to solve it. After moments of frustration and anguish, your brain gives in. It slowly shuts itself down, one function after another, until all that's left are the basic functions to keep you alive.

Your brain hands itself over to your subconscious and there is no separation between your reality and your dreams.

RECREATED FROM SCRATCH

When you sleep the world is recreated from scratch. After you dream and snore and rollover and twitch you wake up to a brand new world. This world may look and feel the same as it did yesterday, but it never existed in the first place.

It doesn't happen all at once and instead begins with the parts of the world that are furthest away from you. It starts with places you've never been, places you've never heard of and places you'll never even know about. They're torn down and reassembled like a cheap, pressboard end table. The land, the sea, the objects, the people that aren't a part of your life and never will be are broken down to the atomic level and then washed away, only to be recreated out of nothing with identical properties, memories and identities.

This invisible force moves closer in from the corners of the world and starts dissecting places that aren't so far away. They're places you've known people to vacation, or that you've vacationed, or have wanted to get away to, or places that your airline alert is waiting on for a price drop. Those places are destroyed and then rebuilt, inch by inch, particle by particle. The force is careful to reconfigure them in exactly the same way they were before. It's happened so many times that there's never a mix-up, the force never slips and no evidence is ever left behind. Even those that know the places you only wish you knew would never be able to tell a difference from one day to the next.

After the world away from you has been recreated the process focuses in on your location and moves in, like an ever-shriveling force field. You start to fall into a deeper sleep and it creeps nearer. It starts with your country, breaking down things that you know and that you're familiar with. National landmarks are torn down, historic sites are destroyed and popular cities are leveled only to be made whole again faster than any known speed. It gets to your state and manipulates cities you frequent and local towns where you have friends, then zones in on your city and rips up the concrete of streets you've traveled and shopping centers you've shopped at and houses you've been inside. It reassembles everything and keeps moving in closer. Just when you're about to be in the deepest part of your sleep cycle, it reaches your house. The neighbor's dog isn't barking because he's being revitalized and the car parked outside isn't the same one you drove to work in the morning.

When that moment in the night comes and you drift off into the deepest sleep your body is able to put you under, the force hovers above your house, spinning like water around a drain. The roof is the first thing to go and the shingles disappear and reappear almost as quickly as the gutters. The kitchen gets destroyed next and your brand new countertops won't be the same when you wake up. The drywall of the living room crumbles and then reappears. The force tears up the carpet and the floorboards and the subfloor and makes quick work of the basement before it moves down the hallway toward your bedroom. It destroys the door on its way in and then hovers above your wooden headboard.

The paper of the book on your nightstand turns into pulp before the nightstand itself is nothing but air. The sheets keeping you warm and comfortable are ripped apart and your mattress is shredded. This is as close to flying as you can get; that one brief instance where everything surrounding you has been destroyed and hasn't started to rematerialize yet. All of this happens while you are lost in your dreams. The force has one more job to do, and it's to recreate you. It focuses in and launches for your body, lying peacefully on the newly-created mattress. You don't feel anything, it doesn't take long and afterwards you don't know that anything is different, but everything is different. The entire world has been destroyed and built up again faster than a bolt of lightning disappears. The force has so much power but now that its job is done it whimpers out until it's needed again. It doesn't go out with a bang, or an announcement, or a show of power, it just drifts away like a rain cloud in the distance.

Don't mistake this weak showing with a lack of power. This invisible, unstoppable force will get the job done no matter what it has to do. If you try to avoid sleep and push the process back, it will start without you. If you wait long enough you might get to see it, but you'll mistake it for a bout of dizziness, visual or audio hallucinations or schizophrenia. It will recreate your world while you're living in it if it has to. The only goal it has is to have a clean slate of the world, a fresh start, every day, and it will achieve it. Just like gravity doesn't care what you do, neither does this force. It will wipe out what it needs to, clean up when it's done and it will do it quietly and quickly while you sleep.

Even though every night the world is in chaos, being crushed and dismantled and revitalized, each morning when you wake up nothing is the same as it was before. You wake up to a fresh world and begin a brand new day.

THE INVENTION OF SLEEP

It started out with good intentions, like most undertakings, but with hindsight it could have been one of the worst things we could have done.

Before the 1900s, nobody slept. It sounds ridiculous, but how would we know any different? Certainly if something was never done, nobody thought to write it down for future generations. For example, no one from today has plans to include a paragraph in a history book that says 'We all do not stand on our heads for 30 minutes in the middle of the day.' Nobody back then thought to tell people they don't close their eyes and snore for eight hours when it gets dark. If our encyclopedias were filled with things that people didn't and don't do, it would be a collection that would have to be updated every minute for the rest of time.

Obviously we all sleep today, so what changed? First and foremost, people started to work more and work longer and the stresses that we know now had begun picking up speed. Cities were becoming larger, more crowded and more people were competing for jobs and a piece of the ever-growing pie. You can probably guess that people started to complain about it all. They went to their doctors and wondered why they were having more aches and pains than usual. A lot of them complained about fatigue, not in the familiar physical sense but rather something that they couldn't describe. Physicians were as confused as everyone else. Some thought everyone was going crazy and others thought everyone was going to die. It was something nobody had ever felt before and it was uncomfortable and new and it wasn't going away. The doctors first saw the issue in men only, but before long their wives started coming in too. Just a few short months after the wives reported it, the children started suffering the same conditions.

The doctors tried anything and everything. They brought back leaches, dull utensils and even went so far as to get rid of soap. As expected, nothing worked. At one point there was a new cure candidate making the rounds that included one bottle of alcohol and 10 jumping jacks. It was soon discovered that the exercise and booze treatment only made the problem worse. Still no one had identified a cure and the list of potential causes kept growing with each new patient and each new case introduced to the equation.

The first actual cure came from a doctor who treated rich clients exclusively. They had the money to try all sorts of things, so nearing the end of his ideas, the doctor suggested anesthesia. He didn't have much of an idea what he was going to do while his patient was under, but the patient didn't know that. So the patient willingly went under and the doctor stared at him, unconscious on the table, and wondered what he could possibly do to cure him. Thoughts of surgery ran through his mind, but the risk seemed to outweigh the possible reward. Instead of doing anything, the doctor sat at his desk and researched potential explanations in his medical books, all the while keeping an eye on the man on his table. Hours had passed and the doctor started to think he had given the patient too much of the drug, but moments later there were signs of life coming from on top of the table.

The doctor rushed to the man's side as he came to. The first words out of the patient's mouth were "How'd it go?" The only thing the doctor could think to say in response was "How do you feel?" It wasn't an answer and it wasn't a lie. The man looked over his body and held out his arms, then extended his legs so that they hovered inches above the table. He said he felt great and the doctor, having done nothing at all, was relieved. The man later sent in his wife and two children to have the same "operation," and it seemed to cure them as well. It didn't take long for the news of this treatment to spread. At first it was just locally, but as words do, they traveled to every corner in every city and soon enough everyone was feeling better and local doctors were feeling richer than ever.

But the feeling didn't last long. The symptoms started creeping back, first into the men, then the women and then it hit the children again, the same as before. Patients flooded back to their doctors, but this time they were more hostile, wanting to know why it didn't work and why they still had this disease. The doctors reacted in a way that should have been predictable, but then again, everything is predictable in hindsight. It was declared that this was a long-lasting disease and treatment needed to be done once a month.

The news was good for some, but bad for others. Not a lot of people could afford a monthly dosage of anesthesia. They tried to make the monthly plan work, but most of the patients stopped treatment after only a few months. Knowing the solution though, many people tried their own forms of anesthesia. Some would drink themselves into a stupor and feel refreshed after recovering from their hangover. Some would have their spouse knock them out with whatever they could find around the house. Some would hold their breath until they blacked out. Some others hung their heads below their bodies until all the rushing blood caused them to pass out.

All of these forms, whether crude and homemade or professionally applied, worked in the short term but the rate at which they had to be applied increased significantly. Once a month lasted for a while, and then people were doing it once every three weeks, then once every other week and one year after this "treatment" was discovered, people were having it done every week, some out of necessity, some just to be safe.

Everyone got tired of the treatments. Some people were running out of money and others just wanted to go one day without their wife hitting them with a skillet (although the wives never complained about this). There were groups formed all over the country that tried to come up with new ideas to solve their problems. A group out of a small town in

Tennessee came up with what we now know as sleep. They suggested that everyone just pretend they had been given anesthesia or were just knocked out and they were hoping that the power of pretend would let them resolve the problem (what we call the "Placebo effect" today). It didn't work for a lot of people at first, they would lay there and stare at the ceiling for hours before deciding they were wasting their time and looked like a fool. But the group pushed forward and encouraged more people to try it. After a couple of weeks, they had their moment. Everyone in the group had been trying it, and it had finally worked. They had successfully convinced themselves to "pass out" for a couple of hours. The news broke so people tried it again and a few more weeks in it started to work for others.

Soon enough this method was everywhere and people were sleeping. It was starting to be prescribed by doctors and was being done in almost every household. The more people did it and practiced it the longer they would stay out. It started at a couple hours and blossomed all the way to max out around twelve. Most people found their groove at around the eight hour mark. This practice became common and kids were starting to be raised to do this. After enough years, it was all the kids knew, and they passed it onto their families and so on and so forth.

Sleep is so built into everyone's culture now that the origins of it have been lost or completely denounced by science. Don't let anyone else tell you differently.

PARTIES

Remember how when you were a kid you never wanted to go to bed for fear of missing out on everything? You thought all the adults had parties and played cool games and did everything you always wanted to do. You were right to be suspicious, because that's exactly what happens.

The minute you doze off, everyone else is up and partying. They're doing all the things you've always wanted to do. They eat finger foods next to ice-sculpture punch bowls and Willy Wonka chocolate waterfalls. They play games you've never heard of, listen to music you can't imagine and swap gifts you've always wanted.

They invite over celebrities and share stories about exotic on-location movie shoots over shrimp cocktails and martinis. The author of the next upcoming bestseller talks details while people browse the fully-stocked wine rack and carry tiny plates of hors d'oeuvres. A top-of-the-charts musician gets inspired while discussing politics by a fully-stoked fireplace clutching a glass of top-shelf liquor.

Sometimes, all that they do is lay low and hang out on the back porch talking about how much they enjoy these times that you're not there.

When you wake up, a signal call goes out to their earpieces letting them know that you're trying to crash the party. They clean up, or just move things out of view until tomorrow night, and scuttle away back to their own homes. Your wife or husband or kids put on their pajamas, making sure it's the same outfit you last saw them in, and climb underneath their sheets and try their hardest to make it look like they're sleeping.

On the occasional day when you wake up in the middle of the night, the signal sounds with an altered tone, notifying everyone that the party is on temporary hold. Everyone scatters and hides, like bugs from a light, while you walk to and from the bathroom or to and from the kitchen to get a glass of water. The ice sculptures and chocolate waterfalls and shrimp cocktails are moved behind the curtains, under the couch or wherever they will fit until the party can resume and you are lost in a deep sleep again. The noise sounds again and your friends, neighbors and celebrity idols come out of their hiding spots and carry on.

Everyone would invite you to all these crazy parties but they know you couldn't keep up with them. You see, you're the only person who needs sleep. It's a weird phenomenon and nobody is sure how it happened, but the world was quick to figure out that you were different, so you couldn't be invited.

You're not alone in missing the parties though, there are some people who choose not to partake. There are some who think it's not fair. There are some who continue to work instead and nobody really likes those people because they make everyone else look bad. They're always working like it's the most important thing in their lives and the party is something they see as a waste of time. They're not mean or angry or upset, they're just party poopers.

They might as well be sleeping too.

Record Setter

Jim wanted to be known.

Jim's problem was that he didn't excel at anything. He ran in the middle of the pack on just about everything. Average at sports, average at music, average at work, average at life. Jim knew he couldn't be known for just being average so he started to look for things he could work on and eventually become more than just average at.

The only thing that Jim could come up with was sleep. He enjoyed sleep, so he decided that it was the thing that was going to set him apart from everyone else, so Jim started sleeping. He read about all the previous sleep-related records, and then he took a nap. He studied the different types of sleep patterns, and then he napped again. He read about the science of sleep, the reason for sleep, the need for sleep, and then he fell asleep. He learned that dolphins sleep with half of their brain still functioning, and then he turned off his brain completely for about three hours.

Jim kept napping and sleeping and napping again until there was nothing to his life except the backs of his eyelids. He lost his job, he lost all of his friends and his house had become a collection of spider webs, dust mites and trash. The only clean part of his living space was the imprint of his body on his mattress. He had become very good at sleeping, so good, in fact, that it was who he had become. He never knew if he was awake or not and he didn't even remember that he had to eat anymore. He lost fifty pounds in two months, then thirty more in two more months and he was now just a living stick figure floating from his bed to the bathroom.

The only thing that snapped Jim out of his trance was an alarm on the calendar on his phone. It buzzed in the middle of the day, while he was napping. It startled him and he was quick to check out the reminder. It said that today was the day the world record recorders were coming over to witness history.

Jim did his best to freshen up, but his house was still a mess and the beard that had grown on his face was crawling its way to his chest. He knew that everyone would understand, so he didn't bother to change out of his worn-down pajamas. He had been awake now for nearly two hours, which was his own personal record for consciousness in the past year. He struggled to stay awake on the couch waiting for the world record people. His head would bob up and down and he'd catch himself every five minutes. His electricity bill hadn't been paid so he stared ahead at a blank television screen, which was far less entertaining than one that flickered with images.

The world record people finally showed up and started setting up their cameras and equipment and were talking too fast for Jim to understand. All he had to do was sign papers when he was told to and stay awake long enough to let them know when he was going to start attempting to break the record. After the last paper was signed, Jim crept his way to the familiar back bedroom, almost falling over from the exhaustion at the three-hour mark. There were cameras mounted all about the room and people standing shoulder-to-shoulder, but he didn't care. People were hooking wires to his head, his chest, his arms and everywhere else they could fit them but he couldn't wait to find that snug spot in his pillow again.

He fell into the bed and wrapped himself up in his gray sheets. He gave a head nod to the man in charge to let him know that his record-breaking attempt was starting now. The man in charge cued everyone else to start rolling and put his finger to his lips to let them know there couldn't be any noise. They all tried their hardest, but Jim could hear the semi-silent clicks of switches and flips. The sounds didn't bother Jim though, he was well past the point of caring. In fact, nothing bothered Jim anymore. His lack of friends, the fact that he didn't have a job, nothing really mattered. The only important thing to him was sleep and he could feel that he was settling in for the best sleep of his life. He dozed off and the last thought to run through his head was how great it would be to finally be someone when this was all over.

The cameras rolled for 12 hours. Crew members came and went. Film was swapped around the 18th hour. More crew members entered and left the building. The man in charge went home and came back the next day. More cameras were brought in. The 28th hour seemed like the longest. At the 34th hour, people started to wonder. The cameras kept rolling and the world record staff hung around, but in fewer numbers. It wasn't until hour 49 that anyone said anything and it wasn't until hour 50 that a doctor showed up.

Rumors spread around town and doctors were interviewed, but there was no explanation. There were a few people who suspected foul play, but the endless hours of film footage proved otherwise. It was talked about throughout the country and eventually spread out across the globe. Jim's death was something that science still doesn't understand but still investigates.

All Jim wanted was to be known.

THE NATURAL STATE OF THINGS

Sleep is the natural state of your body; frozen in time, unaware of its surroundings. When your ticket is called, the Creator pulls you from the shelf and sets you free. Depending on your genetic makeup, or what the Creator had in mind for you, being set free includes a huge range of things and can differ greatly from person to plant to barstool. The only thing that all things have in common is their natural state.

Think of life like silly putty. You can pull the putty, shape it, mold it, form it, stretch it and twist it into anything you can imagine, but eventually it's going to contract back in and you'll be staring at the same shape it started out as. Our life is like that. Every day we get molded into something, or stretched out beyond what we think we're capable of and at the end of it all, we go back to our normal state and sleep it off.

Think of life like a wind-up doll. Every night the Creator spends all of his time going around to everyone and winding them up. Everyone's prepped in their beds, fully wound and ready to go, and when the Creator decides it's time, he lets everyone go, one at a time, just like he imagined. The spring starts unwinding and we go through the day. The spring gets slower and slower and we start to wind down. It finally comes to its final turn and we lay ourselves down to sleep, only to have the Creator come back and wind us up for the next day.

Think of life like a child's toy. One minute it's sitting on the shelf, the next it's being purchased by a parent and grasped by an eager child. The box is open and the toy is moving, interacting with its environment and making the child very happy. The child goes to sleep and the toy sits there overnight, just like it was on the store shelf. It's waiting, motionless, for the next day to come. It finally comes and the interactions start again. Some days are better than others, but every day there's always the end when the toy is sitting there again, motionless and waiting.

Think of life like a cuckoo clock. The first thing you have to do when getting one is to wind it up so that it can run properly. Once it's set in motion it can run uninterrupted for a very long time. Eventually when those chains reach the bottom of their length, someone is going to have to interfere and reset it all so the clock works again. If we're the cuckoo clock, a day is the length of the chain, and the Creator is the one who sets us back up all over again when we're sleeping and unable to keep going.

Think of life like a hot tub. A hot tub just sits there until someone puts water in and starts it up. Only when it's fully running and bubbling with activity is it serving its true purpose. After lots of use though, that hot tub isn't the same anymore. The water is drained and the hot tub goes back to its old, boring, molded-plastic self until someone comes along again and fills it with fresh water. Not only is it a functioning hot tub again, but it's probably better than it was right before it was emptied. Sleep, for us, is like being that empty hot tub. After our day we're totally drained and while we sleep the Creator fills us up again so we can go on to live another day.

Every day we go through this cycle of living, sleeping, being restored and being set free into the world again. However, after enough repetition, we're just not the same anymore. After a long time silly putty starts to crack and is thrown away, a child's toy gets banged up and damaged and is tossed aside, the cuckoo clock breaks and can't track time properly so it's stored in the attic and a hot tub starts to leak and is put out on the curb on trash day. Just like everything else we're all slowly running down with sleep being the only natural, constant, revitalizing state. When all of our living is used up, we revert back to sleep and the Creator puts us back up on the shelf for another time.

THE DREAM MACHINE

Sleepex Incorporated was on the cusp of a breakthrough. Reports had been sent off for scientific review and their "Research and Development" department was already chilling the champagne.

"Do you think they'll find anything?" Charles, the head researcher, walked up to his number one developer and leaned down toward the table where his employee was sitting.

"They'll find that our work is right. I just don't see how they could find anything wrong with it."

"Can I get that in writing?" They both laughed. "Seriously though, we solved that expansion problem, right?"

"Boss," the developer looked up. "We resolved everything. You can stop worrying. You'll be a household name before you know it."

Charles sighed. He knew he needed to relax, but he also knew he wouldn't be able to until the results were in his hands. This was just too big of an accomplishment to react any other way.

"Ha, well, I can dream. All right," he finally said. "Thanks." He was quick to leave the table. He wasn't much of a conversationalist and tried to keep his distance from those who worked for him. He found himself walking back to his office alone again to eat his lunch. Even if his name did become famous, he wasn't sure that would change much.

Charles spent the next four months in his office, reviewing numbers and preparing to report the worst to his bosses and the bosses above them. He knew the chances of the worst happening were slim to none, but that didn't stop him from being fully prepared. It was how he got to his position now and he wasn't about to risk anything.

When he wasn't in the office he was alone with his cat in his two-bedroom loft apartment downtown. It was a nice place, a two-minute walk to the office, and it had gorgeous views that nobody but himself had ever seen. He kept the place spotless just in case that day ever came.

With one of his life goals in sight, he sat on his couch and pondered every decision, every step, every move made up until this point. It was almost exactly how he had planned it out. He worked his way up the ladder until he was head researcher and drove the company for more funding until they had what they needed to complete what the industry liked to call a "game-changing" invention. For Charles and the rest of his crew, that game changer was what they had been calling "Sandman." They had perfected lucid dreaming to a point so much that not only did the sleeper become aware that they were dreaming, but they could control their dreams before and during their sleep states. This was revolutionary.

Their first test case was a subject who had recently lost her dog. After using the "Sandman" and associated medication, the subject reported that she was able to not only see her dog again, but that they played fetch, went on a walk and cuddled in front of the fireplace together and it seemed like she had her dog back for weeks. The funny thing about that was that she was only sleeping for five minutes. The first test for the product could not have gone better. There were minor setbacks when the dreams involved other people, but the team was able to tweak them enough to overcome most issues that test subjects reported.

Charles sat back the entire time and watched it unfold. It started in pill form, but the side effects were too serious to be considered for long-term use and the number of pills a subject would have to take was not realistic in the long run. The team phased out the pills in favor of an apparatus to be worn like a baseball cap. Although Charles preferred an all-pill solution, he knew it was not something they would be able to feasibly achieve. His team went through many different cycles for their new physical apparatus and Charles oversaw all the work. His team was the best in the world from their fields and he knew he would never be disappointed with what they came up with.

Part of the reason he wanted this to become a reality was because he liked the challenge and the idea that it could be done. The other part was because he wanted one for himself. Being so alone was starting to get to the 51 year-old man. He had nobody but his cat and his distant team at work. It wasn't a way to live, he thought. If he could artificially create things closer to him, maybe he'd feel better about it all. He then projected those thoughts onto others who could use the "Sandman" to gain similar benefits. Patients on their death beds, kids with cancer, the elderly who could no longer travel, anyone who has lost someone or something close to them, the possibilities weren't limited.

The day he received the results was just like any other day. He was in his office, going over scenarios and the mail carrier walked in.

"This looks like a pretty hefty package." Anne, the inter-office deliverer, set the package down on Charles' desk. "I think you have to sign for it."

It was rare to have to sign for anything inter-office, but Charles did it anyway. "Thanks, Anne." He said. He opened it, saw the seal of approval at the top and knew that he had to gather his team. They all met in the meeting room across from Charles' office.

"Hello everyone," Charles started. He never knew how to start meetings, he just knew he didn't want to waste everyone's time. "Straight to the point, as usual. We've got the review back and they approved everything. Congratulations!" There were hoots and hollers from the crowd, someone asked where the champagne was, some people hugged while others sat in shock. Charles stood in the front of the room with a giant grin across his face. "I'm going to leave a copy of the approval in the front of the room if you'd like to review it, otherwise I'm giving you the rest of the day off. I'll report up to the board later this afternoon. Congratulations everyone, you all deserve it."

Charles kept his promise and briefed the board members of the results. The paper that the potential profits report was printed on could barely contain all of the 0's which led to a quick approval by all members. With all of the signatures and the gears in motion, it was once again a waiting game for Charles, so he retreated back to his apartment and his cat to do just that.

The products were produced quickly, with all of the company resources at its disposal. It was pushed into the commercial market at the same time corporations and industries were picking them up. At first only the wealthy could afford it. It was priced high and marketed at them and they ate it up. They couldn't get enough of it. Charles' company had to put a halt on orders just to be able to produce more and ramp up the supply. It was an "amazing" product and the reviews were only positive. The elderly loved the way it helped them capture their youth again. People with disabilities could experience things they thought they had lost forever. It was in hospitals and assisted living homes and used in therapy and recovery clinics. It was all going so well and Charles and his team were praised in the media and by the scientific field and were even considered for the Nobel Prize. Charles could not have imagined the scenario to be any more perfect.

But there was a problem.

As the company produced more "Sandman" products the price came down. Every time a price drop was announced, the sales would increase, but the good intention use of the product decreased, at least in Charles' mind.

People who didn't need it were buying and using it inappropriately. Some people started using it to live out their wildest fantasies, or to cheat on their spouse, or to commit crimes and activities they wouldn't normally do because they consider it too dangerous in a normal situation. "Now," said one interviewee on the late night news, "With the risk of everything taken away, I don't need to worry about it." The person had just set up the product and used it to commit murder, living out a twisted dream of his. He seemed like an otherwise decent person. That was the problem though, Charles thought. Otherwise normal people were starting to do the same thing and more and more of them were living in their dreams.

It wasn't a big problem until the price dropped to under $500 despite Charles' complaints. The moment the board members steamrolled his ideas to inflate the price was the moment he pinpointed as being the time when everything changed. It seemed like almost everyone had one, even if they couldn't afford it. There were payment plans, loans, black market deals and a lot of theft in order for everyone to get one. Once people had one they used it all the time and only ever stopped to use the restroom or to eat something. Sometimes they didn't even stop for that.

Everyone had become an addict to their dreams, a slave to the "Sandman" machine. 12-step programs started to popup to try and get people unhooked and back into the real world, but they were mostly empty. Everyone was too busy living out their dreams and fantasies to care about what the real world was doing. Production across the world declined and Charles sat in his apartment with his cat worrying about what he had done to the future of humanity. People were starting to die in the machine he created because they were so wrapped up in the phony world they were forgetting to take care of themselves. Even when they stepped out of their dream worlds and back to real life, people would often become so depressed that they couldn't continue on. The suicide rate jumped and only a few media outlets noticed.

Real life conversations were empty and day-to-day activities weren't exciting or new. Charles and team didn't even consider this in their wildest thoughts about the product, but now they were here and their invention was slowly killing the world. Birth rates dropped and death rates increased and everyone could see where it was going, but too few people were looking at it to care. Soon enough the people who cared and tried to change the course of humanity gave up after accomplishing nothing and plugged themselves in as well. It was the first sign of mankind's white flag.

Charles and his team tried to solve the problem, they tried to come up with a way to reverse what they had done, but it was way too late. There was no going back now. What they had given couldn't be taken away and they knew their time was up.

"Well, we had a good run." Those were Charles' last words to his coworkers. That night he walked back to his apartment. He played with his cat for a while before she got bored and wandered off, then he took a shot of whiskey and went to the corner of his living room where his personal "Sandman" was unplugged and had been un-used for most of its life. He gave a deep sigh, leaned down and plugged it in. It whirred to life while he popped a pill. He decided he wasn't going to look back. He sat down, setup what he wanted the rest of his life to look like and started dreaming.

Can't Sleep

Brittany couldn't sleep. She thought it was because of the caffeinated iced tea she consumed at dinner, but it could have been her boyfriend's dead body in the basement.

She had been staring at the ceiling for some time now, the clock said it had been an hour and a half, but to Brittany it felt more like a week. The longer she looked at the texturized paint, the more shapes she started to see. An elephant in the corner, an ice-cream cone next to it, a knife over here, a blood splatter in the corner, a basketball by the window.

She was tired but didn't know what to do. When she was younger she'd call out for her mom to be cuddled to sleep. Being 28 and nine hours away from her parents she figured that wouldn't work as well this time. The dead body might also make her mom a less-than-willing participant. She turned her head to the side and saw that it was now three in the morning. All of the bars were now closed and there was officially nothing to do in town.

She sighed.

She watched the minutes melt away on the digital clock for a while and then got up and slouched over to the kitchen. She had to step over a chair to get into the kitchen and tiptoe around broken glass to fill her glass up at the sink. As her cup filled the splotches of red on the stainless steel bounced around inside her water and it looked like they were floating in her glass. She shut off the faucet, danced through the glass, stepped over the chair again and walked into the dining room.

The table used to be organized with placemats, napkins and a one-year anniversary flower arrangement, but the vase was now shattered, resting in tiny shards on the floor and the flowers were wilting, spread out throughout the room.

She took a sip of her water. The moon outside was gorgeous and full. The light bounced off of it and into the dining room, lighting up the slivers of glass like little crystals. It reminded Brittany of the bracelet her boyfriend gave to her the night they celebrated their anniversary at the Italian restaurant downtown.

She started to wonder if she had made a mistake. She wished she could just get some sleep and deal with it in the morning, but that didn't seem to be in the cards tonight. Although, she couldn't imagine that anything that happened tonight was in any cards anywhere. She shrugged off the thought with another drink of water. It was bound to happen at some point, she had seen signs of it before tonight but didn't want to admit to them. She had suggested treatment, he had suggested therapy, but tonight nobody suggested anything. There was still an empty beer bottle rolling around the living room floor, propelled by the train passing in the distance.

If she had dealt with this earlier then it wouldn't have all boiled up like it did tonight. She knew it was a problem, she just never thought it would get this bad. Her water was getting warm the longer she sat there, but she still wasn't tired. Her heart had finally stopped racing, but it wasn't quite back to normal.

He should have done something, she thought, as she tried to pass the blame on to the victim. But you were the one that had to take action, another thought flickered across her brain.

"We could have solved it." She was talking out loud now.

"We did, that's what tonight was; a solution."

"You just hate me, don't you?" The glass in her hand was shaking.

"I did what was best for us."

"Best for us? You mean best for you, you just want control." The glass shook even more.

"I *have* control."

"No you don't!" Brittany tried to control the shaking glass, but something overcame her and the water poured out onto the floor. She threw the glass across the room and its pieces joined their vase counterparts and widened the ever-growing sea of crystals.

"You can't stop me now. You were right though, you had the chance."

"Shut up, shut up, shut up!"

"You should have listened to your boyfriend when he suggested therapy. You only have me to listen to now."

"I won't." She yelled as she ran back down the hallway and into her bedroom. "I'll show you who has control."

"What are you doing? You can't."

Brittany tripped on the exchange from wood floors to carpet when she reached the room. She started crawling and searching for the knife she had seen earlier.

"I can, I'll show you."

"You would never."

She reached for the knife in the corner.

"You can't have me anymore."

"No!"

Brittany dragged the edge of the knife against her wrist.

"You stupid bitch!"

Brittany didn't hear her imaginary friend; she was too busy concentrating on avoiding the pain. It hurt, but not as bad as she thought. She had been through pain before, and compared to that, this was nothing. She set the knife down on the carpet and leaned up against the bed. She had accepted her fate and she was okay with it.

Finally, she thought, she would get some rest away from the voices and the anger and the hate. It was the most peaceful she had been in years.

INDUSTRY

Over a lifetime a person will spend around half-a-million dollars on sleep-related products. This includes mattresses, pillows, sheets, blankets, beds, alarm clocks, sleeping pills, pajamas, snore strips, relaxation CDs, white noise makers, sleep masks, ear plugs and everything in between.

Industry-wide, mouth guards alone counted for nearly one billion dollars last year.

Pillows are the most frequently purchased items and account for almost 20 billion dollars annually. There are so many categories of pillows that the manufacturers classify them incorrectly 35 percent of the time. On the last industry-wide audit there were more types of pillows than there were breeds of cats. One house alone contains, on average, over 10 different types. There are body pillows, contour pillows, decorative pillows, bath pillows and aromatherapy pillows. There are also soft, hard, and in-between pillows. There are throw pillows, feather pillows, massage pillows, overstuffed pillows and pillows with speakers. Also in the list are travel pillows, pet pillows, inflatable pillows and neck pillows. How many types of pillows do you have?

Sheets are the second-most purchased items and bring in around 18 billion a year. There are lots of types of sheets too, but they don't have nearly the diversification as pillows. Sheets stake their claim to second place despite the lack of regulation for them. If you took the time to actually count threads you would notice, more often than not, a disturbing trend of inconsistency. You think your sheets actually have a thousand threads? 800? Six? Sheet thread count tends to be off in a negative way, by 20 percent. The manufacturers love taking away threads, but there's never an error in your favor. Remember that the next time you go shopping and are about to pay an extra 60 bucks for more threads. You can't tell the difference anyway, can you?

Beds are a huge money maker but only come in third due to the relatively low rate of turnover. The industry tried to speed it up by making claims about how your bed doubles in weight over eight years, but that's just marketing nonsense. A bed can last as long as you want as long as you take good care of it. However, beds still tend to have the biggest research and development team and their ability to crank out new products is really incredible. These are the innovations like memory foam and the ability to change the stiffness with the push of a button and even water beds. Innovations that aren't included are often the extra padding on top or the "pillow top" beds (more pillow references!) or any bed with a heating or cooling element.

Clothes are next in line with an easy 15 billion dollars-worth of material sold every year. That revenue is split with pajamas at the top and pretty much everything else vying for a sleeper's attention. Comfortable socks are included along with robes, slippers, gowns and the infamous "headwear" category ranging from mouth guards to snore strips to sleep masks.

Food and medicine are gaining in popularity with more and more people being prescribed sleeping pills, while alarm clocks are dropping off the charts at alarming rates. The drop in the graph for alarm clock sales coincides perfectly with the sharp rise in smart phone usage worldwide.

To justify spending this much everyone knows that saying that a person will spend at least a third of their life in bed. That's another marketing trick to make you buy more fancy pillows and upsize your mattress. It's okay though, they know you're not going to do the math anyway. Halfway through they figure you'll want to go lie down and try out your new "Thermo-insulated SuperSoft Arometherapeudic Blanket with Down-stitched edges." You bought it, but you have no idea what half of it means or if those are even real words.

I've run all the numbers and I've checked and in the end it's all marketing nonsense. I've submitted my ideas to scientific journals, medicinal boards and even government agencies, but no one will hear me out. They've all got their ears plugged with cash from the lobbyists in Washington. They may be able to fool most of the people, but not me. I'm writing this in hopes that it will find you someday, a person I don't know, have not met and will probably never meet, but someone who will know the truth. They want your money and they're willing to do whatever they can do get ahold of it. Remember this for the next time you go shopping and see some fancy new sheet designs or pillows advertised as being even more comfortable than you could ever imagine. Most of the stuff you don't need, you can do without, and there are more important things to spend your money on.

Like coffee.

Like fast food.

Like another set of dishes.

Like a new shower head.

PATIENT 3

"How's number three look?"

"Better than yesterday. His brain activity has leveled out and it looks like he's hit REM."

"Perfect. Shock him."

"But he hasn't slept in days," the man at the desk pleaded.

"That's why we're here." The lead researcher wrote a note on his clipboard and looked back at the man running the electronics for the experiment. "Go ahead."

The man sitting at the board hesitated and then pushed the yellow button marked "Electrical Shock." It was cruel, he knew, but he was warned when he signed up for the study. The two men could see patient three on a black and white screen labeled "Three" on the desk in front of them. Patient three jolted out of bed and threw the covers onto the floor. Patients one and two were sound asleep in separate rooms.

"Why?" Patient three's weak voice came through the speaker next to the television set. He turned around and pointed to the camera in the corner of the room.

"Why won't you let me sleep?" His voice sounded desperate, but the lead researcher said nothing and instead wrote another note down on his clipboard. He viciously crossed his "t" and looked to the other man in the room.

"These are good results, don't you think?"

"Are they? I don't know as much about the study as you."

"What's there to know, really? We're just finding the minimal amount of sleep someone can get before snapping."

"Why, exactly, is that important?"

"I don't know, okay, it's just what the person who gave us the grant wanted us to do."

"But isn't that —"

"Don't ask too many questions, okay? Just give him the puzzle."

The man at the desk sighed. Next to the "Electrical Shock" button was one with a "Puzzle" label. He pushed it and on the TV he could see part of the wall in patient three's room flipped around to reveal a puzzle. It was a logic puzzle, one of those games where you have to find out who did what in what order and what item they did it with. It wasn't too hard, but when you were going on less than four hours of sleep in four days it proved quite difficult.

Patient three had finished it in five minutes the first day. For day two he clocked in around six and on day three his time had already dropped to 18 minutes. Yesterday, he didn't finish the puzzle in the allotted 30-minute window. He finally got around to it at minute 43. Today didn't look promising for a new record.

The lead researcher and the man at the desk watched patient three struggle with the puzzle in front of him. Patient three completed it in just less than two hours.

"I didn't think it would be that bad." The man was jotting more notes on his clipboard paper.

"Well, what did you expect?"

"I'm not sure really." The man finished his notes. "Make sure you keep him awake, okay? I'll be back in 15."

"Got it." The man at the desk watched the clipboard disappear.

The electronics board on the desk had over 30 buttons with only two labels. The lead researcher never questioned why there were so many buttons with so few labels, but it wasn't important to his goal. The man at the desk, however, had a different goal. He pushed a third, unmarked button and a light came on in patient three's room.

"Is he gone?" Patient three asked.

"Yes." The man at the desk replied.

"How's it going?"

"You tell me, you're the one going through all this."

"It's worth it." Patient three was staring right at the camera.

"Is it?"

"I've gone to great lengths to find out how the human mind works and the empathy that it can produce, or in our case, not produce."

"What if he ends up killing you?"

"That's why I hired you, isn't it?"

"True." The man at the desk paused. "I couldn't let that happen anyway."

"If he lets it get that far though, then we'll have the best results I've ever experienced."

"If that's how the human mind works, I'm not sure I want to be in this field anymore."

"I just want to let you know that you should always be prepared for anything." Patient three, the person who provided the grant, the person who orchestrated the grand study, the person who wasn't a patient at all sat down at the edge of the bed. "Because sometimes, that is exactly how the human mind works."

Thanks to the Gremlins

When you're sleeping the gremlins in your brain come alive. They only have one task and they do it very well. They go from place to space in your grey matter, grabbing memories, determining their importance and storing them in the appropriate filing cabinets of your mind.

They run across to the far reaches and find that memory you have from the second grade where you forgot your lunch and had to sit in the cafeteria trying to mooch a carrot off someone. It's a good lesson, they decide, but it's time to be archived. They grab it and rush over to storage where they have to determine where to put it. Should they put it with other second grade memories? Maybe it should go with memories about food, or carrots, specifically. The gremlins talk amongst themselves and decide to file it away with second grade, so they do and then they run back across to decide the fate of the next thought candidate.

The second memory they pull is more recent, but not very important. It was a Sunday afternoon in the spring and you had to run to the store for a few things, so you threw on some clothes and headed out. You didn't know this at the time, but it was much hotter than you expected outside and you wished you would have put shorts on instead of pants. This is not an important memory, so the gremlins run back to put it into storage and classify it with other temperature-related memories rather than grocery shopping or pants.

The next memory the gremlins pull is the first time you tried smoking. This memory is available to be archived, but the gremlins decide that it's too important to leave behind in the dark recesses of the brain, so they leave it, ready to be accessed at any time, ready to have an important impact on your life again if the time arises.

The gremlins spend the entire time you're sleeping running back and forth and all over the different levels of your brain, determining memories that need to be archived and leaving the ones that are too important to be pushed out of the limelight. There are millions of gremlins too, because you have a staggering amount of memories and the gremlins need all the help they can get. Since there are only a finite number of gremlins, as you age and acquire more memories they have a harder time archiving them all. The quick-access section of your brain gets cluttered and messy and memories start to get tangled and intertwined, which makes it even harder for the gremlins to separate. It's like putting a strand of lights in a box in the attic and pulling that strand out years later only to find that it's tangled itself into a knot. It takes time to undo, and the more knots you have the harder it's going to be.

After enough time has passed, the gremlins get tired too, because they have memories of their own but no one to clear them out. The gremlins get even slower and bogged down. Memories get missed or archived incorrectly. The gremlins can't keep up. The only way you can help them is to sleep and give them more time to sort everything out, so as you get older, that's all you start doing. When the "big sleep" comes, the gremlins have more than enough time to sort all the memories and get them all in order. They spend months and sometimes years getting it all corrected and when they're done, they die off, finally satisfied that they have completed their life mission.

And when you're in the afterlife, the instant they're done and all of your memories have been sorted, your entire life history becomes crystal clear and things are more vivid than ever before. It's all thanks to the gremlins.

POSITIONS

The position you sleep in at night will directly affect your decisions the following day. It's like reading a horoscope, but more accurate. If you can record the different positions you toss and turn into while you sleep, you will have a pretty good idea of how your day will go. For example, if you sleep on your back for the first half of the night, then on your side for the rest, you'll have a normal morning followed by a more creative afternoon. The following is a list of 12 positions and their likely impact on you the next day.

On your back, arms crossed or at your side: Your day will go mostly as normal and follow your usual routine. The decisions you make will be typical choices, the conversations you have won't be too far off the normal mark and you will have an easily forgettable day. You will eat cereal for breakfast.

On your back, arms up by your head: Your day will be normal but you'll have more of a sense of dread than usual, as if you were giving up. You'll want to punch your boss in the face on more than one occasion. Someone you know will almost die in an unlikely and equally stupid way, like almost choking to death on a grain of rice.

On your left side, legs and arms straight: You will have difficult decisions to make and will spend a large time trying to figure out the best outcome. Your day won't be easy but you'll find it more rewarding than usual. You'll think more before you speak and your choices will seem more logical than usual. You will be closer to solving a Rubik's cube on this day than you ever have before.

On your left side, legs curled and arms tucked: Your decisions will be more difficult than normal but you won't have trouble dealing with them. Your decisions will lead to the expected outcomes and you will generally be happy with all of the results. Your lunch will contain an unexpected spice and you'll enjoy it.

On your right side, legs and arms straight: Your day will be crazier than usual and this will cause you to see things through a different perspective. You'll think about your future more and how you want to get there and what you have to do to achieve your life goals. You probably won't eat cereal for breakfast, but waffles are a good possibility.

On your right side, legs curled and arms tucked: The perspective you see things through will open up new opportunities and you will take them. Every decision you make will be marked by a moment of learning and understanding. You will suddenly comprehend the solution to all of life's problems only to have them flee your mind when you get a random phone call from an unknown number.

On your stomach, gasping for air through the corner of your mouth with your arms by your side: You will wake up in a pool of your own drool and the day won't get any better from there. Your toast will be burnt, your car will break down and someone will steal your seat at some point in the day. Make sure you always carry an umbrella with you after a night sleeping like this.

Your face in the pillow and your butt in the air: You will be confused about everything the entire day. You may think that you've suffered a stroke but you haven't, the blood that rushed to your head all night is draining and your body is adjusting. You should sit down in a comfortable chair for at least an hour before attempting anything strenuous.

Sitting in a chair: You will spend all day tired and wishing you could find a bed. Once you find a place to rest, you won't be able to fall asleep. Also, your neck will hurt.

Standing: You need to see a doctor.

Face down on the floor: You will wake up surrounded by liquor bottles and everything around you will be dirty. You'll be wondering all day what the day before was like and you will never find any answers.

On your stomach, face down smothered in your pillow: You will wake up dead. As a side note, this will be the only time you sleep in this position.

SLEEP WALKERS

Ted had always been a sleep walker. Nobody knew about it until, at age seven, his parents found him urinating in their closet. They told him it was okay and that it happened to everybody. That wasn't the first time Ted had been lied to and it certainly wasn't the last. From that day forward his parents attached a bell to his door and every time it rang, they were quick to spring out of bed and catch Ted before he could stain something other than his bedroom carpet.

Tiffany was also a sleep walker. Her outing was less embarrassing than Ted's. Her sister found her watching TV at two in the morning but found that they couldn't have a coherent conversation. She was scared and woke her parents only to find out that her sister was sleep walking.

Ted had another sleep-walking moment when he was spending the night at a friend's house in junior high. They had all stayed up late and played video games and around three in the morning they all crashed on the floor of the basement, television still tuned to late-night infomercials. About a half an hour later Ted fell into his normal sleep-walking pattern and got up and wandered around the room. Luckily he managed not to pee on anything, unluckily his best friend's sister had a room further down the hall, and as fate would have it, that's where Ted headed. As you can imagine, it didn't end too well. Ted's parents were called and explanations were had and the cops were never called, but he ended up going back home that evening. Ted and his friends couldn't have any more sleepovers but they stayed good friends. Ted needed a good friend, because as soon as the rumors about him trying to sleep with his best friend's sister spread through the school he started to lose some friends in different circles and found himself to be the butt of many jokes. Ted wasn't happy, but the rumors tapered off the minute that someone in the eighth grade got pregnant and became everyone's new target. Ted had survived, but he didn't like the fact that he had to live with this condition.

Tiffany's sister would try to get out of trouble and use her older sister's sleep-walking condition to her advantage. Tiffany took a lot of blame for breaking valuable things around the house, cutting the dog's hair, painting the walls and other childish nonsense. When they were older the blame turned to things like sneaking out late at night, stealing money from their parents and even smoking pot. Tiffany's parents were never sure what was going on and punished both of their kids to hopefully steer them in the right direction. In school, Tiffany and her sister had reputations that they were rough around the edges, but Tiffany hated it. She tried to excel in school but could never shake the rumors of her sneaking out of her house at night to smoke with one of the "bad boys."

Ted kept himself mostly out of trouble until college. The first major incident was when he happened to be dating a woman who lived in the all-girls dorm across campus. He was spending the night there, and almost as if the gods had a personal vendetta against him the sleep walking kicked into gear. He was woken up in the middle of the bathroom by the hall resident advisor. Needless to say, she wasn't too happy. He tried to explain it to her, but at four in the morning it was hard to get anybody to listen. He was threatened with expulsion but the medical card he acquired before attending the school saved him from any such punishment.

Tiffany had an equally rough time in college. Her freshman year she had tried to pull an all-nighter to study for a Psych exam but must have fallen asleep somewhere around the chapter on states of consciousness. She woke up on a bench outside the entrance to her dorm. People had gathered around and thought she was a passed-out drunk. The first thing she saw was a group of people pointing and laughing. It was a terrible way to start the year.

The second major mishap that happened in Ted's college career was two years after his first. He and two of his closest friends had an apartment just off campus. The apartment was part of a large complex which often hosted parties in the courtyard area, usually with kegs and underage consumers. The cops were at this complex almost every weekend, which should have been a sign that Ted was meant to stay away, but he never realized it. On one chilly fall evening, Ted wandered out to the courtyard, or as it was more commonly referred to, the "Partyard". It was later described to him as being a shoulder-to-shoulder crowd and he wondered how he ever even managed to not wake up in its midst. But Ted didn't wake up and as anyone could have predicted, the police arrived. Since Ted was out of it and could have very well been mistaken for a drunk, he was quickly cuffed and hauled off to jail. He came-to in the back of a police car which was one of the scariest moments of his life. A blood-alcohol test and his medical card got him off the hook once again, and the police apologized and he had to hoof it all the way back to his place where his roommates proceeded to give him a hard time about it all the way to senior year.

Tiffany's life didn't get much better after her first incident. A year later, in all of her sleep-walking glory, she couldn't figure out how to get down from her loft, so she managed to fall face-first into the carpet-covered concrete and break her nose. Her roommate jumped out of bed and drove her to the hospital where she stayed overnight. When she got back home she didn't want to leave the room again, but eventually figured she couldn't miss all of her classes. She walked around campus for the next two weeks wearing a giant, white bandage around her face.

This was how it went for Ted and Tiffany. This was their life. He graduated and got a job and moved on, all the while suffering through his sleep-walking condition. She graduated in three years, eager to get out of school and back to the real world. They both took medicines and sleep aides and tried numerous things to get rid of it, but it always managed to stick around. Ted and Tiffany met just one year after graduating at a sleepwalking support group.

They dated and conversed about their sleepwalking troubles and laughed together about it. They had both never been able to relate to someone so much and they had never been happier. They went on to get married and have children, none of whom suffered the same fate as their parents, which was a surprise to both of them. When they got old their kids moved away and then one year for Christmas all of the kids came back. Their oldest presented them with a gift from all of the children. Ted and Tiffany opened the package and found a movie inside.

They watched it and they started to cry. The kids couldn't be happier. All the while that they were growing up, they secretly recorded their parents sleepwalking, events that neither Ted nor Tiffany knew about until this Christmas morning. What the kids captured had truly made these unlikely sleepwalking partners believe they were meant to be together. The first movie they watched was a sleep-walking Ted and a sleep-walking Tiffany eating a meal together at the dinner table, seemingly having a meaningful conversation, although their words were just gibberish. The next clip showed them dancing in the living room to music that was only playing in their minds. The movie jumped to another time when they had both sleep-walked downstairs, put in a movie and were cuddled on the couch.

The movies went on like this until the tears in Ted and Tiffany's eyes made it so they couldn't see anymore and the kids turned it off.

THE WORST NIGHTMARE

Dave bolted upright, afraid and confused. He leaned against the headboard and tried to catch his breath. His heart was racing and sweat was dripping from his forehead. He wiped his brow only to find that it didn't help; his hands weren't any drier than his face. This nightmare was the worst one yet.

The horrendous dreams had been getting worse and worse since the end of summer but he had no idea why. He thought it had been because of the stress at work, but once his big project settled down the dreams didn't get any better. Tonight proved that the nightmares were not improving.

His wife was still asleep underneath the covers next to him. He didn't want to wake her again after already having done that far too much of late. He'd wake up in the early morning, jolting up from the bed which would wake her up too. She was a light sleeper on normal days, so any disturbances would mean she'd be up for at least an hour. It took her some time to get back into that sleep mode once she was awake. On several occasions she had decided just to get up and not even bother. Dave felt terrible. She was a hard-working woman who already didn't get enough sleep, so every time he made it worse he felt guilty.

He stared at her all cozy and comfortable and thought about what it would be like to sleep soundly. He threw back the blanket so that it only covered his legs. He hoped it would help the sweating. After a few minutes of sitting in his bed, half-covered in a blanket and listening to his wife's silent snores, he got the chills and wrapped the comforter back around himself.

He was feeling better, his heart had slowed and the sweats were mostly gone. He didn't want to go through that again and was afraid of having another nightmare, but was more afraid of not being able to get any sleep. He was teetering at the four-hour mark and if he fell asleep at this exact moment he could get in three more at the most. He slid back down the bed and rested his head on the pillow.

"Feeling better?" His wife asked.

His suspicions were confirmed. Maybe she had tried hard to fall back asleep, but somehow he knew he had made too much noise and moved around too much.

"Sorry I woke you." Dave replied.

"Bad nightmare again?"

"Worse than the others."

"You want to talk about it?" Dave's wife turned to face him, still hiding beneath layers of sheets and blankets.

"Well I saw myself, from a third person view, like a camera just over and above my shoulder, you know?" Dave could just make out the shape of his wife's head in the dark and talked toward it. "And I was wearing these weird clothes.

There was a long, skinny blue rope around my neck. It looked like someone had tried to hang me. I was walking along this endless row of square-shaped rooms I guess, but they didn't have any doors, you could just walk right in. All of the rooms had one table and one person, and the person was staring at one of the walls. It was almost like they were trapped in there."

His wife sat up a little more and Dave continued talking.

"Then I came across a room that was empty and stared at it, I must have been a prisoner or something. Then a couple more people wearing nooses stopped in my room and yelled at me, and this happened the entire time, and I couldn't leave."

"That sounds like torture." His wife said.

"Exactly. But it gets even weirder. The next thing I know I'm in the middle of a street, and I'm in another square-shaped box and I'm surrounded by people who are in their own boxes. We're all just sitting around in the street in our boxes, like prisoners again. Every now and then we seem to just float a few feet ahead, but mostly we just sit there. And more people are yelling but I can't hear them, I can only see them, and they look angry. Then the person next to me starts yelling, at me this time, and then I'm awake."

"Are you sure you're feeling okay?"

"I will be, but just talking about it made me start feeling weird again."

"Get something to drink and come back to bed. Maybe that'll help." His wife turned to kiss him before rolling back over to catch up on sleep.

Dave set his feet on the lava floor and it felt nice and warm, just like always. He shuffled to the window and then jumped out. He landed in the middle of the city in time to see the mayor wrestle a mountain goat, as was typical before the sun rose. There were some spectators, but he had seen it numerous times so he kept shuffling. He skirted down the street into a hardware store that was covered in snow. Dave didn't like that his wife kept the kitchen this cold. He reached up onto the top shelf of the first aisle and grabbed a pitcher of green liquid.

He took a gulp out of the pitcher and put it back on the shelf. It felt good, but he didn't know if it would help him sleep or not. He walked back out the door and the streets had changed. Dave was now in a cave. It meant the mayor had won the fight. He hooked in and climbed his way up a far wall, passing blue and orange lights embedded in the rock. He unclipped himself at the top and walked out of the cave into an open field.

There was a giant Sasquatch behind him, so he started running. He didn't think the Bigfoot would be out this late. His run was more of a slow-motion, stuck-in-syrup run, but the Sasquatch never caught up to him. He ran out of the field and was now standing in front of his house door. He opened it and stepped inside. There was nothing for his foot to hit, so he fell. He fell for a long time. Eventually he landed on a bed of glass, but it didn't hurt. He got up and brushed himself off. Their elevator was waiting here, so he took it up to the ninth floor where his wife was, still trying to fall asleep. He walked back into the lava-covered room and headed for his side of the bed.

"Feel better?" His wife asked, still not asleep.

"A little. I just hope I don't have that nightmare again."

"I'm sure you'll be fine. Goodnight."

"Goodnight, honey."

The Couch

Well, here I am on the couch again. I've grown quite used to it actually, after having spent a ridiculous Tracy-only-knows how many days here. I could probably cope with it better if those days were consecutive, but instead I have to guess whether or not my wife is going to let me sleep in the bed with her every time I walk through the door.

I've thought it possible that she has some sort of bipolar disorder, but the times when things are going good she seems so normal. It's odd how one person can flip around on you so much without any warning signs. Of course if you ask her she'll say she gave me warning signs longer than she had to, ergo why I end up on the couch. If you ask her she'll say I never get the hint and don't know when to apologize. That's all if you ask her. If you ask me I think she's just making things up and this is some kind of twisted test. It's probably because she's been talking to her sister again. I think our marriage would be better without sibling gossip, rumors and women's magazines.

This is another time where I don't know what I did to deserve another night on the plaid, mid-90s pullout sofa. At first I assumed it was because of our tussle about the garbage disposal, but when I brought it up she scoffed and said I didn't know her at all. Looking back on it, I should have kept silent and let the disposal incident fade into memory where it had almost been anyway before I resurfaced it. That was the biggest argument I remember having in recent times. Of course we disagree from time to time, like loading the dishwasher or putting our "Thank You" cards in the mail, but nothing ever escalates beyond the back and forth that ends in easy submission (typically by me) after about 30 seconds.

I'm sure it's all just a misunderstanding. I'm the one missing and she's the one understanding. That's always what it is and it's getting on my nerves. I've tried to ask her multiple times to explain it but she keeps repeating the "You don't listen to me" mantra and then trying to talk to her is like talking to a brick wall, except the wall would express more empathy.

But it's fine, I guess, late night TV isn't bad. The worst part is that I never get good sleep out here. We could upgrade the couch, but she won't let me spend money on it, she thinks it's unnecessary, but of course she's never had to sleep on it. So I'm here watching *CSI* reruns and I know my wife is stewing in her own anger in our comfy, multi-hundred-threaded Egyptian-cotton sheets. She probably won't get any sleep either, but for totally different reasons. At least I get to enjoy TV and she has to sit in a dark room.

Maybe I'm being hard on myself and maybe she's getting the real punishment. Talk about twisted; I'm sure I'm twisting something in my favor.

The night carries on, mostly as expected, and I finally grow tired of watching detectives solve cases and say witty punch lines. Either that or I've seen every episode so many times I know exactly what's going to happen; if only my wife worked like that. All I know is that Tracy and I will fight and I will end up on the couch. I don't know the beginning and I don't know the middle part, all of which are kind of important. There's just no rhyme or reason to it, at least on *CSI* there's mostly a form of order in the double-rape-underwater-homicide cases. If only my life were so simple…

I finally decide to call it quits and turn off the TV in the middle of a gripping investigation. I grab the quilt from the hidden ottoman drawer along with one of the scratchiest pillows known to man. This thing is rougher than me after two days of not being able to find my electric razor. I'm not sure how we acquired this pillow, but I'm starting to think Tracy got it on purpose, knowing that someday I'd be forced to use it to try and get some sleep with. If that's the case, she's smarter than I give her credit for.

The quilt is okay, but it doesn't keep me very warm. I'd turn the thermostat up but that would just extend my sentence by at least two days, so I keep it where it is and try and pretend like the scratchy pillow is some sand and I'm in the middle of the desert. It's a good plan and it would probably work except for the blue glow emitted from our DVD player that's brighter than most peoples' headlights.

I'm too comfortable now to get up and cover it with anything, so I just stare at it, hoping to intimidate it into being less fierce, but it doesn't work. It doesn't work just like it didn't work last time, or the time before that, or the time before that, or any time ever.

I'm lying on the couch, feet extended past the arm rest, covered in a not-so-warm quilt with an itchy-as-sandpaper pillow being blinded by this DVD player power button and I'm contemplating why I'm in this situation. I keep running myself into circles and it feels like I'm starting to make things up. Was I forgetting entire conversations? Were days going by where I just didn't listen to my wife? Is that what she wants me to believe? Do the suspects on *CSI* question themselves as much as this?

I'm sure this is what she would want me to do, to question things and try to figure it out in my head, but I just can't. I'm tired, I want to sleep, I want my brain to shut off like she often claims that it does, but I think tonight is proof that it just can't be done, even when my body and spirit are willing. By now I'm sure she's fast asleep, dreaming up some punishment for our next fight that includes an even worse sleeping condition, but for now the current punishment is fine. I'm just not sure the treatment fits the crime, whatever the crime is.

In a couple of short hours the sun will be up again and I will have to face another miserable day, but for now I'm starting to think that I'm crazy. Maybe my wife doesn't even exist and I'm making the whole thing up. What if I were crazy? What if I'm in a mental institution and this uncomfortable pillow and worthless quilt are standard-issued items? What if the blue DVD light is some kind of research mechanism? Are they getting the results they want?

Just when I think I'm onto something big, a huge breakthrough, I wake up. My leg is cramped, my foot is asleep and I'm sure there are lines all across my face. The DVD light doesn't seem as powerful in the early morning glow of the sun, but the pillow is still rough. I sit up at the edge of the couch and try to make my foot stop tingling and once it does I head toward the kitchen to make a pot of coffee. I stare out the window at the sunrise and wonder if I wasn't on to something when I thought I was crazy. That's when I hear my wife come into the kitchen.

"Good morning," she says, wearing her plush slippers and fluffy robe. "How'd you sleep?"

I pause and stare at the coffee dripping into the glass pot. Is this some sort of cruel joke? What about another test? Was this something she read about in one of those stupid magazines? How was I supposed to respond? What was the right answer? Then I start thinking that maybe I am crazy after all. Did I just dream the whole thing? Why is she going on like nothing happened? Usually she's still angry in the morning and nothing makes sense, why the change? I feel like I'm being cornered, like a dog who's been digging in the garbage, making a mess in the kitchen and is backed up against the stove with a table scrap hanging from his mouth. The more I think about it, the more I think there isn't a right answer, so I go down a route I normally wouldn't. In a typical conversation I would response with either "Good" or

"Not good," but I know in this case that those responses will only make it worse. I look up from the coffee pot and see my wife standing in the doorframe waiting for an answer, so I gamble.

"Did you want any coffee?" I think it's a safe move and with it I've avoided all the traps I normally get myself into. I try to anticipate any responses she could send back, but I'm not sure what they would be. I'm hopeful in my newly-acquired ability to flip the tables and I'm now the one waiting for an answer from her.

"So you still don't know what you did, do you?"

With that reply, I know I'll be spending more time on the couch. I also know that there is no way out. When my wife is upset with me, she is going to win. It's useless to try and do anything else. I don't respond, which I know is going to make her angry, but I've realized it doesn't matter anyway. I pour myself a generous cup of coffee and carry it with me back over to the old-fashioned couch. I can hear Tracy getting angrier from the kitchen, but I don't really care. I turn on the TV and find another rerun of *CSI*. I sit back, sip my coffee and settle in because I know it's going to be a long ride.

The Experiment

They figured out a way to watch us dream.

At first there were critics, saying it couldn't be done, that it shouldn't be done and it was a waste of everyone's time and resources. Just like the Wright brothers heard, but look at where planes are today. That's what spurred on the research. "It could open doors," some said. "We could understand so much more," was a saying thrown around a lot too. But they failed to realize the negative and instead focused on the positive, much like how no one could have foreseen planes being used to eradicate entire locales and populations. They just wanted to get there from here in the air. All researchers wanted was to see what people were dreaming about.

They accomplished it earlier than they expected. It was only five years into the research and their initial plans were to have this kind of breakthrough around year seven. They thought it was a mistake at first, but they re-ran the tests and verified that they had indeed uncovered this breakthrough. Third parties were brought in to validate the claims and scientists from all over the globe ran the experiment on their own terms. After one year of letting everyone else at it, the scientific community was 100% behind the discovery, an unprecedented acceptance rate that gave legitimacy to this new technology.

At first it was used just to gather information, they wanted to see what it was that people were dreaming about. They marked trends and patterns and information and tried to map it all together based on populations, characteristics, personalities and a whole host of other data. The data was studied around the world and myths were debunked, like spicy foods make you have bizarre dreams and everyone dreams in color and you have hundreds of dreams every night but you don't remember them.

The field of psychology was fascinated with this new technology and was an early adopter. They had machines in all of their offices and it was one of the first things new patients had to go through. There was a booming field of "Dream Analysts" who claimed that they could tell you everything you ever wanted to know about your subconscious based on this "life-changing and amazing" new technology. Some of it was real and some of it was made up for effect, but people bought into it and the new "Dream Machines" made their way into popular culture.

That's when things started to get weird.

The paparazzi claimed to have videos and images from the dreams of celebrities and scandal sales were higher than they had ever been. Presidential candidates were asked to hook themselves up to the machine so that people could see the "real" them. One of the candidates dreamt about having an affair with his secretary, and when a follow-up investigation turned up some real evidence of the affair, the "Dream Machines" suddenly turned into a subconscious lie detector.

The machines were now in the courts and used as admissible evidence. You had to provide a weeks-worth of dreams to your employer just to get hired. All dreams a month prior to your flight had to be cleared by the government in order to travel by air. Dream information was sold to marketing firms and they used it to try and sell you more crap you didn't need. The phrase "In your dreams" carried actual meaning. The madness didn't stop; the machines had become part of everyday life.

The scientists who let this technology out into the world warned people that it wasn't how the machines worked, they didn't tell the truth or predict the future and to use them in that way would be to abuse the technology beyond its original purpose. But people didn't listen. Before you got married the state had to approve your dreams to be sure there wouldn't be a divorce or domestic abuse in your future. Before a couple had kids they had to submit to dream evaluations to be sure they would be fit parents. There were random inspections of your dreams to be sure you weren't going to commit any crimes, and if any evidence was found that you would even consider it, you'd be hauled off to jail.

Soon enough the streets were empty, nobody was married and the child population plummeted. The great advancement was causing the world to slowly die off.

It was something nobody had ever dreamt of.

How the Other Half Lives

When you go to sleep, somebody else wakes up. They might live on the other side of the planet, or they might live right down the street, the universe doesn't care. The universe is just trying to keep a balance. It's all about balance.

That one time you fell asleep in church, a man on the other side of the aisle woke up from his quick nap. The old man was quick to nod off again and that was when you jerked your head back and became embarrassed that you couldn't stay awake for the preacher's sermon.

When you were fully awake, that man was sleeping, but his wife was quick to nudge him back into the lecture of original sin. At that moment, a woman across town fell asleep lying on her couch watching a rerun of an *I Love Lucy* episode. She woke up two hours later when a movie started rolling that had a higher volume than the classic TV sitcom. She kicked off her blanket and nearly fell off the two-foot high sofa.

The moment that woman's blanket landed on her carpet, a baby in the house across the street closed its eyes and fell asleep for its mid-afternoon nap. In one hour the baby was crying and screaming from its crib, suffering because it didn't know where it was or if the woman who rocked it to sleep was ever going to show her face again.

While the baby was screaming and crying, another person in another time zone was sound asleep for the evening. After having washed the dishes for the night and laid her children to rest, she was gone as soon as her head hit the pillow. She was dreaming of what her life would be like if she had only waited to have children, instead of rushing into it.

The woman kept dreaming and halfway around the world, the sun was just beginning to rise on the horizon and a man woke up after a long nights sleep. He was getting ready for a long day of work, 12 hours was what his boss said, but it would probably end up being closer to 14 or 15. He had to get to work first thing in the morning just to fit everything into his day, to get it all done, and still make it home in time for another round of sleep.

16 hours later he was back home eating dinner and before he knew it, he was headed back to bed again. It was one of his favorite places because when he slept, he didn't have to think about his job or the rest of his life, or lack thereof. He threw on his old shirt and pants, brushed his teeth and fluffed his pillow. He set his alarm clock an hour earlier than the day before and rolled over onto his side and drifted off into the comfort of sleep.

As the warm and familiar embrace of sleep grabbed the man, you were just waking up, more than half a world away. You didn't care about the troubles of the man who was universally linked to you, but even if you did, it would be a different man, woman or child the next day. You were blissfully unaware and you woke up and ate a pastry.

This is how it goes, every day, all day, for as long as humans have inhabited the planet. Nobody knows how it started, or why it's like this, or even how it will all end. Do death and life count toward this balance as well? Will we ever know, or is that something so far out of our grasp that we shouldn't even bother to think about it? If we die is someone else born? If a new baby enters the world, does an old grandmother have to leave? If that's the case, why are there more people being born every year? How is that balance? Are we all linked, or are there some who fall out of this inexplicable ripple effect?

These are the things human think about while they're awake. But everything is forgotten about when we lie down and rest and instead, someone else is waking up and taking on the burden. Maybe this is the way it is just so that the conscious of the universe never falls asleep. Someone somewhere is always awake, just to be sure the universe doesn't cease to exist.

Narcoleptic

Susan had no problem sleeping, literally. She was a narcoleptic and fell asleep whenever the condition struck. It proved itself to be quite inconvenient.

Her first memory of her condition was in the second grade. She remembers Ryan Trauder showing off his brand new remote-controlled car and then she found herself being woken up by the teacher. Ms. Knott had a pained look on her face and sent Susan to the school nurse right away. After a few more incidents like that there were memories of doctor's offices and hospitals and gowns and scans and medicines and frequent naps.

It wasn't until she was 10 that she understood why she was weak and tired all the time and slept so much. It wasn't until high school that she fully comprehended what this meant for her getting older, not to mention having a relationship. She went out on a couple of dates and tried not to bring up her condition until the third dinner at least. Most guys were okay with it but others didn't want to have to deal with someone who was "broken."

Many boys crushed her heart and to even think that someone else considered her "broken" was traumatizing. Her parents tried their best to reassure her that she was perfectly normal, but that only got as far as any other conversation with a teenager. She was depressed and started binge eating. The problem she soon discovered was the extreme emotions that made her want to eat also triggered her nervous system and she would fall asleep soon after they kicked into gear.

Susan gained weight. Between her binge eating, constant sleeping and inability to participate in sports or activities at school there wasn't much she or anyone else could do about it. Her parents became worried and sent her to a psychologist hoping to pump some life and excitement into their young daughter and get her to act like everybody else, but it was no use. She would go to her sessions, but never get anything out of them. From Susan's perspective, it was a waste of time. There wasn't anything this man with a PhD could do for her. All she had was her constant medication and piles of food to keep her somewhat stable.

Her parents would drive her everywhere, which only further embarrassed her, but she was constantly reminded that it was far too dangerous for her to drive, so she had no choice but to get in the passenger seat and hope nobody saw her. Her food eating continued with her psychology sessions all throughout high school and by the time graduation rolled around, her parents were seeing improvement and were hopeful.

They had such a good outlook that college attendance was thrown around in conversations over the dinner table. However, her parents wouldn't consider anything other than the state college 30 minutes away. They said it was for her own good. Even that, they said, was a huge risk. She tried to convince them that she could handle being on her own, that she would be fine, but they never budged and Susan settled on the state college.

What she didn't tell them though, or her psychologist, was that she was as miserable as ever. She had realized a while ago that the only way she was ever going to live a real life was to pretend everything was okay. But it wasn't. Susan wasn't strong enough to handle her disease by herself, but she thought she was. She thought she could make it in the real world, without anyone's help, especially her parents. She believed so much in herself that she thought she could make it in Hollywood. She would land acting parts and become a national hero for others with her condition. She wanted to help raise awareness, she wanted to give others someone to look up to, something that she never had. Most of all she wanted to finally be accepted after years of rejection and embarrassment.

She never told anyone what she really wanted. That's why it was such a surprise to everyone when they found her out west on the interstate a couple of hours from her college. She had veered off the road, most likely due to an attack, and crashed into the median.

Her friend at school said she asked to borrow the car for a quick trip to the grocery store. Seeing as how the store was only a two-minute drive, she thought there wouldn't be any harm in it. When she didn't come back, her friend got worried and started calling people. Eventually the police got involved and the interstate crash was tied together with the missing person case.

In a cruel twist of fate, now Susan is the one who sleeps uninterrupted and her parents are up all night, sleeping odd hours of the day and generally miserable.

GIRLFRIEND

"Why don't you ever stay here?"

"What do you mean?" He slipped into his sneakers by the door.

"You always leave." She tiptoed from the hallway to be closer to him. "Why do you always leave?" She leaned against the wall and let her oversized shirt fill the gap.

"Sorry babe." He leaned in and kissed her on the cheek. "You know I can't stay."

"That's what you always say, why can't you just stay once?" Her face was pouty and she batted her eyelashes. He was too busy putting on his coat to notice. "Can't you just sleep here?"

"You know I would but I have to get up early and I don't want to disturb you. Plus I snore and I know you wouldn't like that." He turned around to open the door. "Plus, you can't miss your beauty sleep, right?"

"You think I *need* beauty sleep?"

"No." He pulled his hand off the door handle and swung around. He grabbed his girlfriend by the hips and pulled her in close. "You know I don't think that. You're

- 74 -

beautiful." After a passionate kiss he grabbed for the door handle again.

"I know," she said, reeling from the kiss and letting her mind wander to earlier in the night.

"Love you babe." He opened the door and stepped out onto the landing.

"Love you too." She blew a kiss at him but the door was already closing. She went to bed not knowing what her boyfriend actually did at night.

He walked back to his car and pulled away from the apartment complex. It was getting easier and easier for him, but he knew it couldn't last forever. There would be a time where she wouldn't accept his lame excuses and he would have to make a choice between his typical night routine or having her, and he knew it would be a hard choice.

It wasn't that he didn't love her, it was just that he loved his job and it paid extraordinarily well. With his education he knew he could never get a job that paid anywhere in the same ballpark as where he was now. It was a tough job, and he was warned ahead of time not to get himself a girlfriend. Others in the business told him it would be tough, probably impossible, and that he would be an idiot to pursue it. Being young and dumb he went for it anyway and now he could see it was going to bite him in the ass.

He drove down the familiar streets and the houses got more expensive the further north he travelled. It was a nice perk of the job, similar to the pay, but it wasn't anything he looked forward to by any means.

He knew his girlfriend wouldn't approve, and in fact, would dump him, spread rumors and never speak to him again if she found out. He considered the legality of his job as a giant gray area, but he knew it was definitely a morally questionable profession. He didn't tell anyone what he did, but in having casual conversations about the topic with friends, family and acquaintances he knew how people felt about it. There weren't too many people that accepted it, other than those in the field, but that was to be expected. It wasn't glamorous, most of the time it wasn't fun and sometimes it could be embarrassing, but somehow it was addicting and he just couldn't let go.

He pulled into the driveway of a three-story Victorian home and parked on the right side, behind the third stall in the four-stall garage. He parked his car, hopped out and walked up to the door. He knocked five times and waited. It was a nice night out, but not nice enough to make him forget his girlfriend he was leaving behind for this.

He was at a crossroads, something he rarely encountered, and was forced to make a choice. Just the simple fact that he was here right now instead of with his girlfriend should have told him what he actually wanted, but he couldn't bring himself to believe it. He kept telling himself he could quit anytime and for the past seven times he had told himself it was the last time, but here he was again, waiting outside of the familiar house.

The door opened and a face he had seen dozens of times was staring back at him. It was a woman in her 50s with graying hair, obvious sagging facial features and a body shape that must have been considered a 10 in her prime but was now closing in on a four in a fast way.

"Ms. Egger." He nodded his head.

"I told you to call me Jenna when we're not in public."

"Sorry, Jenna."

"What took you so long?"

"Sorry, you just live pretty far out here…"

"Well I'm not paying you for the drive, okay?"

"That's fine." He stepped inside and took off his jacket. Before he could even hang it up, Ms. Egger grabbed him and kissed him.

"I hope you came prepared, I want to try some new stuff."

"I'm always prepared, Jenna."

"Good, let's go."

Before following his client up the stairs he thought about his girlfriend, asleep in her bed and dreaming about her perfect boyfriend. If only she knew, he thought. He hesitated for a moment and Ms. Egger turned back from halfway up the stairs.

"What's the problem?" She asked.

"Nothing." He shook off the thought of changing his life momentarily and remembered the payout. This'll be the last time, he thought, and followed Jenna up the stairs.

BRAIN VACATION

When you sleep, your brain literally goes on vacation. It packs its belongings in its suitcase and heads out the door.

Most of the time it stays local, but on occasion when it gets adventurous it likes to travel to places that your body isn't willing to go. It'll pay for things you normally wouldn't and sign up for activities your body fears. Your brain craves excitement and if it doesn't get it throughout the day it wanders off at night, free from the shackles of your flesh.

It goes bungee jumping, rock climbing, kayaking, deep-sea fishing and hiking. It travels by hot-air balloons and rides ostriches and hitchhikes out to the Grand Canyon. It'll wrestle alligators and complete a triathlon and finish a hot dog eating contest. It does everything it's ever wanted to, all while you're sleeping. It's no wonder that your dreams are so weird. Your brain could be halfway across the world, slathered in sunscreen, donning sunglasses and a wide-brim hat hiking across the desert all while you're clutching your pillow and drooling on the sheets.

All of our brains are all over the place doing these things, but people don't care, as long as they're nice and polite and pay the bill, which they always do. The brains don't talk much, mostly because they're busy processing all the information around them at the same time that they're keeping your slumped body alive underneath the covers. They awe in wonder at the sight of the Nepalese mountains and tell you to keep breathing. They gaze around the vastness of the Pacific Ocean and tell your hand to scratch your leg. They are mesmerized by cultures that have only been exposed to them by books up until this point, then they tell you to roll over because if you stay in that position your back will be in terrible shape in the morning.

At the end of the day for them, it's the end of night for the rest of you. They double-check their suitcase to be sure they didn't forget anything and they start heading for home. On their way back they go through the painful process of purging all of their recent memories. They can't hold onto the jungles of South America, or the yacht race where they finished second place, or even the spelunking they did in Mexico. None of the memories can stay, so they all get lost on the trip back. That's why it desires to leave every night in the first place, because even though it's done all of these things, it never remembers them.

And your brain is sad, because all the adventures, all the trips, all the exotic locations that it's been to and seen, it knows there's not a good chance it'll be back. It wants to bring you, for the full experience and so that it can hold onto what it's forced to lose. It wants you to touch, feel, see for yourself and remember the Trans-Siberian railway, the ruins of the Aztecs and the claustrophobia that overwhelms when you're on a submarine. But it knows it probably won't be able to convince you, and the only way it has to do these things is limited to a small fraction of time at night.

So your brain drags itself back home and unpacks all of its belonging before purging its last memory. It jumps back into your head and tells you to wake up.

TRUE HAPPINESS

Bethany and Harold met each other in kindergarten.
Harold was new to town and Bethany was the social one in
class, at least for a kindergartener. She was quick to share her
toys and eat lunch next to the weird, new kid. She and her
friends sat next to Harold until he could buddy up with
some of the other boys for the reading circle every afternoon.
Even after Harold found his own group Bethany still wanted
to sit next to him every day. After the reading circle she and
Harold would lay out their mats for nap time and fall asleep
next to each other underneath the cloud-painted ceiling.

This was the first sign they were meant to be
together.

Bethany and Harold grew up around each other and
their friendship only got closer throughout the years. Their
parents set up play dates with each other and some other
kids from the neighborhood. Their bond grew stronger
through this extra time and any rumors of coodies by either
Harold's or Bethany's friends were easily dismissed because
they had known each other for a while. By the time the fifth
grade rolled around they were having sleepovers at one

another's house. Their parents didn't see any harm in it and would even let the kids sleep outside in an old, raggedy tent. The first night in that old tent they talked until they were so tired they didn't mind the cold, lumpy ground beneath them.

This was a moment they would reflect on as they grew older.

For Bethany and Harold, middle school was where things really started to change. Bethany and Harold were still strong friends, but their own circles were gaining influence and the time they spent together lessened every day. They would still converse in the halls and talk back and forth, but the days of sleepovers were long gone (much to the parent's delight) and there were only a few instances where they had the same lunch hour together to be able to eat their sandwiches side-by-side.

This was the first time either of them realized how much they enjoyed being around the other person.

Bethany and Harold were in a complex situation in high school. After many attempts at dating what Harold deemed to be "the wrong woman," he decided that he would best be matched with Bethany. After all, he thought, they were good friends already and knew almost everything about each other. What could go wrong? They tried dating a few times with little success and were officially labeled the "on-again, off-again" couple throughout school. Their reputation was so famous that even the teachers were taking notice and placing bets on their relationship status. They were officially "on" going into graduation, but because they were parting ways to attend different schools they had to split up. Even though they both tried to convince one another at some point that they should stay together, in the end they knew that it would never work. Before graduation they decided to hang out one last time, "for old times' sake."

This was the first time they ever slept together.

Bethany and Harold lost touch with one another throughout most of their college careers. They were studying at different schools, in different states and were home so infrequently that even if they wanted to touch base they wouldn't have been able to. Probably for the better, they both thought. They didn't have anything in common anymore other than a shared past. The problem was, they both thought that, and didn't discover it until winter break of their senior semester. They ran into each other at the grocery store and found out they would both be accepting jobs at the end of the year in one of the big cities nearby. They decided to go out that night and catch up. After a long evening of coffee and dessert they agreed that they should try and make a relationship work.

This was the second time they ever slept together. And third.

And fourth.

Bethany and Harold both started jobs in the city and lived in separate apartments on the opposite sides of town. They would make detailed appointments and carefully craft their calendars to see each other the maximum amount of time that both their jobs and their commutes would allow. They started doing everything together and integrated one another into their friend circles and even started hanging out with couples their own age, some married, some single, some already divorced. For both of them, it felt like kindergarten all over again, minus the reading circle and nap time. They were seen together everywhere and their friends joked that if they invited one, they'd have to invite the other. They were a package deal known collectively as "Berald." It didn't bother Bethany or Herald and their relationship grew stronger as they grew older.

This was the first time they realized they were meant to be together.

Bethany and Harold got married after almost three years of being together. The wedding brought a lot of old friends back into their life and even gave new life to some existing ones that had started to fade. They became an example of love for a lot of people. They had their arguments, like all couples do, but their foundation was so strong that it held up to any test put up against it. Their friends were in wonder as they watched Bethany and Harold's marriage survive the years as others got married and divorced and re-married.

This was the first sign that they were going to be together forever.

Bethany and Harold had two children, a perfect set of girls. They were two years apart and were raised to be each other's best friend. Bethany had her idea for raising children and Harold had his, but they were able to compromise on most of their teachings. Their girls were involved in sports and music and school activities and their parents struggled to stay on top of it all. Between their own jobs and the girls' activities, Bethany and Harold hardly had time for one another, but they always managed to set aside at least some time every week to re-affirm their lifelong commitment. The girls looked up to their parents, even though they wouldn't admit it in junior high or high school, and they flowered under their guidance. Both of the girls were eventually off to college and Bethany and Harold had an empty house and an empty bank account.

This was when they realized they had grown up together.

Bethany and Harold were in a weird phase of their life. Just like when they were younger, it was just them and they had all the time in the world. They used it to get to know each other again. What had they missed about the other person while they were raising their girls? They went on dates again and stayed out at night even though that meant coming home earlier than they used to. They had deep, meaningful conversations about life and what it meant to each other. Their conversations on similar topics in the past never seemed so powerful and meaningful. They continued to get to know one another as their daughters married upstanding men and grandkids started to show up. One year for Thanksgiving they were gathered around their daughter's table about to dine when they looked up and caught each other's eye.

This was the first time they realized they had grown old together.

Bethany and Harold couldn't believe how far they had made it in life and how quickly the time seemed to have passed. They were slowing down and couldn't do everything they wanted to do anymore. Their daughters eventually had the visits and discussions about moving into an assisted living center. Bethany and Harold were both strongly against it at first, but in the end they admitted that it would probably be best for everyone. They moved into the center and it wasn't as bad as they were expecting. They still had their car, they still went out and they still had fun. They wondered why they hadn't done this earlier. They met even more friends at the center and a lot of them were in the same situation. Everyone had visitors all the time and it was exciting getting to know and meeting new people.

This was better than expected.

Bethany and Harold kept the conversations going, but the physical activity was almost non-existent. Their daughters came to take their car away, Bethany got a walker and Harold got a cane. It crept up on them and they hadn't seen it coming. They were still happy, just disappointed that they were nearing the end of a very long, very successful run. They would mostly stay inside and sit at their respective chairs, watching daytime TV until the clock told them it was time to go to bed. They'd eat at the cafeteria at the designated time and take their pills shortly after. They started needing help doing simple tasks like bathing and going to the bathroom, and soon enough there was a full-time nurse around to help whenever they needed. Their daughter's visits grew further apart and they got to see their grandkids even fewer times than that.

This is when they realized this was where they would be at the end.

Bethany and Harold had reached the end of their life, but there was nothing to be sad about. They talked about it and wondered why they were still around. Most of their conversations were based around that same topic, at least when they could have conversations. Either one of them was sleeping or their hearing aid wasn't turned all the way up. They carried on like this until their bodies couldn't take it anymore. They had been moved to separate twin beds in the same room now to make it easier for the nurses to move around, but one night, Harold leaned over Bethany's bed and maneuvered himself into a lying position next to his wife. They were both still on the bed, staring up at the ceiling until Harold turned his head and whispered into his wife's ear.

"You know I love you, right?"

"I know, dear." Bethany whispered back.

"I always have."

"I know."

There was a moment of silence as both of them had tears rolling down their face. They knew there was nothing left for them here and they wanted a final peace. They knew if the mind was willing, it could overcome anything. They grabbed each other's hands and squeezed until they couldn't squeeze anymore. Bethany had tears pooled at the corners of her mouth.

"I love you." Harold whispered through tears.

"I love you, too." Bethany whispered back.

This was the night they fell asleep holding each other, not knowing whether they would wake up, but always knowing they would love each other until the end of all time.

KAREN

Karen is a third-grade math teacher. She spends her days standing at a whiteboard teaching eight and nine-year olds how to do simple multiplication and division problems and trying her best to get them to understand decimal places and most of the time her efforts are worthless. The kids that go to this school don't care. They aren't slow or disruptive or have learning disabilities, they're just lazy. They care more about what's going on outside the window instead of learning the difference between the tenth and hundredth decimal place.

She spends her nights and weekends trying to figure out a better way to teach the children. She tries to come up with neat activities and interactive demonstrations they can do, but when the time comes to do them she is forced to pick people to assist, and when she pulls the kids to the front of the room they manage to turn off their brains entirely. There are two "good" kids in the classroom and always want to help, but if she picks them all the time or calls on them exclusively the other kids zone out even further.

She's tried movies and games and speakers and prize giveaways but the motivation simply isn't there. When she has parent-teacher conferences she realizes that the situation starts at home and the kids are only displaying the same lazy attitude that they have learned from their parents. In her five years of teaching she has only seen the kids and their parents get worse and worse and blame her for lousy performance more every year.

Karen's reached out to the other teachers at the school, asking for advice and tips, but she only receives brush-offs or mild laughter and a questioning look when they pass one another in the hallways or the teacher's lounge. It's not that the teachers are unfriendly or want Karen to fail, it's just that they have been in the classroom for such a long time that they no longer have the desire that Karen expresses every time she asks them for help. They see it inside of her and it only makes them more resentful and hateful of what got taken from them. It's not Karen's fault, it's just the way that things go, but Karen doesn't want to end up like the teachers that surround her.

She's brought it up to the principal, the superintendent and even the school board, but they're so busy trying to get funding just to keep the history textbooks up-to-date that they tell her it's a good idea and that something should be done about it and give Karen the task of coming up with that something. Karen writes proposals and researches techniques in her free time, only to present them to those who asked and eventually get turned down because of "lack of funds to implement new teaching methods."

Every day when the last bell rings, Karen wonders if she got through to any of the students that day. She packs her things up and hopes that she still has time to make a difference in their lives. She's starting to get frustrated and isn't sure if there's an end-game to this at all or if it's all for naught. She tosses her bag in the passenger seat of her 1995 Toyota Camry, notices the near-empty gas tank and wonders if she has enough in her account to cover a full fill-up. She ends up only filling halfway and praying that she can make it at least one more week without stopping at the gas station. When she gets home the only thing waiting for her is an individual Healthy Choice meal and her cat, Nathaniel.

"How was your day?" She asks Nathaniel, filling up his empty water dish. She knows he can't respond, but she at least hopes he'll show some affection. Instead, he prances to the new water and takes a sip. "Mine was fine, thanks." She continues as she walks to the only bedroom in her house to slip on her comfortable sweats.

She throws her lasagna in the microwave and plunks an old *Gilmore Girls* DVD in the player. She presses pause when her single-serving meal is ready and waltzes back to the couch only to find Nathaniel has taken her seat. She moves a pillow from the cushion beside her cat and sits down.

"You always get the best seat in the house, don't you?" Nathaniel doesn't respond, as expected, but he does look at her for a brief instant before putting his head back down on the cushion he recently stole.

Karen finishes four episodes of her favorite show along with a couple of glasses of wine before deciding she had better get some sleep. While she brushes her teeth she stares in the cleaner-streaked mirror and wonders if her life will ever change for the better. She knows she's trying to make a difference in the world, but she never expected it to be this much of a challenge. She starts to think that maybe it isn't worth it after all.

She sets her alarm and slips underneath the covers. Nathaniel is quick to follow and snuggle next to her in her double bed. It isn't great, she thinks, but it's by far the best part of her day. The moment before going to sleep, to her, couldn't get any better. She's comfortable, she relaxes, she knows she has a loving pet and suddenly everything feels better. She feels recharged and ready to make a difference again. It's moments like this one that keep her going.

She falls asleep happy.

CLARITY

That instant right before you fall asleep is the moment where everything becomes clear and reveals itself, you're just too out of it to know. Your minds makes millions of connections a second about everything that you've been thinking about, and a millisecond before you fall asleep, everything is revealed and you are enlightened.

It's a known effect that people have been studying for years. It's the reason people will say "sleep on it" regarding a big decision, because your brain will make up its own mind, whether or not you realize it is another matter. Those connections you make microseconds before falling into a deep sleep have a reverberating effect and at least some of them will hang around. They'll stay in your mind while you sleep and pop in and out of awareness. Sometimes you'll dream about them, sometimes you won't. Even if you dream about them you may not remember it when you wake up, which is the true pain of it all. Your brain is capable of solving and sorting millions of problems but more often than not, doesn't have the capability to recall the solutions.

Imagine your mind like the sun. The sun is up all throughout the day, shining on everything and generally available (minus some clouds from time to time). This is you when you are awake. You're there, going through the motions, but constant from one day to the next. After a while the sun starts to set and it gets darker and darker. This is you later in the day. You're still there, doing your thing, but you're getting tired and fading. When the sun has set and is gone for the night, it's dark and we won't see it again for a while. This is you when you're sleeping. Not much (that you are aware of) is going on, even though the sun is still there and actively working.

Now imagine a sunset. Between the act of falling and being gone completely, the sun has a few minutes of brilliance. It lights up the sky dramatically, revealing vivid colors and leaving a wake of wonder in its way. The spectacle only lasts a few minutes, if you're lucky. In the overall timeframe of the day, those two minutes are only a fraction of the whole but they're the best part. Those two minutes are like the two microseconds before you fall asleep. Connections are made, your brain is clicking away and working harder than ever and makes everything look so beautiful. But before you know it, you're out, and it's dark.

Your brain is smart, it really is. You think you're smart, but it's really your brain doing all the work. It can solve complex situations when it's running at high speed, but if it were to run at that speed all the time it would burn itself out and you'd be a walking bag of meat. So it chooses the best time to do that, the time right before the body rests and it knows that it'll be working less and there are fewer things to control and worry about. You are generally going to try your hardest at the end of the race, when the finish line is in sight, rather than at the beginning, especially if you don't know how long the race is going to be.

So your brain is figuring everything out for you and storing it somewhere, it's just hard to retrieve. You may think that's unfair, but that's how it is. You can try to move all of those revelations to a time when you'll remember them, but I doubt you'll have any success. Your brain is smarter than you, so good luck trying to trick it and get around its self-imposed limitations. But if you plan to try something, before you go through with it, just make sure you sleep on it.

UNABLE

I can hear you, Jeff wanted to say, but he couldn't say anything.

He had been trapped in his body for three months, not knowing how it would turn out in the end. Jeff could only count the days by when his family came and went. Sometimes they had gifts, sometimes not, sometimes they were crying, sometimes not, but each time they would say something to him.

"Happy birthday, Dad." His daughter leaned over and whispered into his right ear. She placed a gift wrapped in polka-dot paper on his bedside table and retreated back to the protection of her mother's legs standing at the foot of the bed. His wife reached up and dabbed the corner of her eye with a tissue, careful to mask the action from their teenage son staring out the window. It was especially hard for Jeff's son, to witness his vulnerable father sprawled out on a hospital bed. *Cheer up, bud,* Jeff would say, if he could. He knew he probably wouldn't be there for his son's football games, or to teach him how to tie a tie for homecoming. Jeff hoped he wouldn't be out that long, but from the sound bites of doctor speeches that he got drifting in and out of sleep, he couldn't be sure.

"Happy Halloween." His wife was standing next to the bed now. "The kids are out with their friends and I wanted to spend the night with you." She walked over to the TV hanging from the top of the ceiling at the front of the room. "So," she continued talking as she bent over and picked something up off the chair from underneath the TV. "I thought we could spend it like we used to. Scary movies and popcorn." She flipped open the DVD case and slid the plastic disc into the integrated DVD player. She hit play and the first *Halloween* movie came to life. She walked back to the side of the bed with a bag of popcorn and sat down in the plush seat next to Jeff. He could hear the opening credits of the movie and he knew when his wife was digging around in the bowl, grasping for not only popcorn but lost memories of time spent with her husband. It brought him back to happier places and if he had the capability to cry, he would have.

"Happy Thanksgiving." Jeff's wife and kids walked in with bags of food. They pulled up TV trays to one side of the bed. His son sat facing the wall, his wife sat in the plush side chair again and his daughter sat on the bed since there was just enough room for her. They all reached toward one another and held hands. His wife slipped her hand underneath the blanket and found her way toward Jeff's lifeless fingers. "We give thanks today for our family. We give thanks for Dad, who is still here with us and will soon be able to be with us again…" His wife carried on with the prayer, but Jeff zoned out and became focused on the word "soon." Whatever it meant, it hadn't happened fast enough. After the prayer Jeff could hear the sounds of everyone dining on their meals. He imagined turkey and cranberries and cornbread just like they had every year. He wished he could take in the smell of fresh rolls and gravy again, even if only for a second. He would have cried if he could have when his daughter, mid-chew, leaned in close and whispered "I love you."

"Merry Christmas, Daddy!" The kids came running in first, his daughter with her green pants and red shirt and his son with a Santa hat on. His wife trailed behind with bags of wrapped packages, cookies and decorations. The decorations were the first agenda item. Jeff laid there and thought about previous years where he would climb into the attic to get the tree, hang up the lights and put ornaments in the yard. He wondered if his son was still carrying on the tradition or if it was too hard for him to seemingly "replace" his still-breathing father. Jeff started feeling guilty and found himself wanting to cry again.

In under an hour the family turned his bland, uninspiring hospital room into a winter wonderland. A tiny tree decked out in Christmas balls stood tall on the tiny table in the corner while frost clung to the window and fake snow covered nearly every surface. Streamers and garland were wrapped around chairs and hanging from the TV and oversized stockings were falling off the edge of the bed. Jeff's wife put out a plate full of cookies and served eggnog to everyone who wanted some. They spent the evening singing carols and some of the nurses came in to partake as well. Jeff singled out his wife's amazing voice and it gave him more hope than he had ever had before. He was convinced that he could will himself out of his current state and found that this moment gave him more strength to be able to do that.

The evening ended with the gifts. The kids opened theirs first, just a couple, and none of which were from Santa. His son got a videogame and the always-exciting clothes. His daughter received a new doll for her collection and a self-locking, electronic diary she had been clamoring for ever since before the accident. His wife's only gift was from the kids. The wrapping paper was torn and creased in the wrong places and if you looked hard enough you could see what was underneath. Jeff was happy knowing his son had taken up the responsibility that normally falls on the father. He knew his son was trying, and that was more than he could have asked for. Jeff felt guilty again but he was glad he had taught his son well enough so far in his life. His wife opened the odd package and revealed a nice mug and a package of hot chocolate. She thanked the kids and then got up to get a gift for Jeff.

"Now, I know you can't open it," she said walking back to the bed, package in hand. "But we'll help you." She placed the gift on the bed and she opened it with the help of her daughter. As his wife was opening it she said, "I know you probably can't enjoy much, but I'm hoping we can do at least a little to help out." They got the package open and it was a set of flickering candles. "They're the same ones we use in the house, and I know you probably can't smell them, but it sounds just like the ones in our basement." She placed them on the bedside table and lit the tall one. It wasn't the smell of cinnamon that Jeff noticed but rather the crackle of the wick as the flame came to life. The only other flickering candle he knew was at home and he was glad his wife had thought of it. The smoke rolled through the room and the aroma brought another holiday touch to the stale hospital room.

"And," his wife said, lifting another package from the floor. "I don't know how much they'll let you use this, but I'll see if I can talk them into a deal." They went through the same routine of opening it and revealed a stereo system. "It hooks into your MP3 player, which I just so happen to have brought." She pulled out his years-old player from her purse. After opening the stereo box, and setting it up with the help of their son, she slipped the MP3 player into the audio jack, hit shuffle and Jeff's favorite music began streaming through the room. It was the greatest gift he could have asked for. Long gone were the days of trying to decipher the conversation in the room next door, or count the number of cars he heard drive by outside his window. *Thanks,* he wanted to say and cry, but all he could do was lay there.

His wife came for New Year's Eve and she once again decorated his room, this time with streamers, confetti and balloons. She talked to him all night long about how their kids were doing, how the extended family was taking the news and most importantly to Jeff, how she was handling it all.

"It's hard," she said. "It's really hard. Sometimes I want to give up, I just do." She turned and looked at Jeff and started to cry. "I just, never thought I'd have to go through this, you know? I was never prepared, how do you prepare for something like this? And then it just hits you and changes your life, changes everyone's life." She dabbed at the corner of her eye with a tissue. "But I want to be strong, I have to be strong, for the kids."

You are strong, Jeff wanted to say. *You've always been strong, that's one of the reasons I love you. I believe in you, I know you can do it, and as soon as I'm better we'll be a team again.* Jeff wanted to cry out to his wife and support her, he wanted to let her know that he would always be there for her and love her. Unable to move, all he could do was listen with his eyes closed and it tore him up inside.

"I feel like this is my fault too, you know? I mean, I was the one who drove you away and practically put you in that car that night. I should have just handled it all better, I should have been able to do that. I'm just mad at myself." Her tears of sadness turned into those of anger and, out of instinct, she turned her back to the bed.

It's not your fault, Jeff wanted to say, but he couldn't say anything. *And I love you.*

The man on the TV counted down from 10 and the people in Times Square celebrated when he reached zero. Jeff's wife, wearing a silly, pointy hat, leaned over and kissed her husband on the forehead.

The visits continued but, for the most part, slowed. Sometimes the kids came and sometimes it was just his wife. Sometimes everyone was happy and sometimes they were all sad. His wife still showed up angry from time to time but sometimes she was stronger. For Valentine's Day she brought cupcakes and near the end of the school year she brought in pictures of their son's Prom and their daughter's school year and set them on the end table. The summer break caused lots more visits by the kids and they had good, long conversations with their father, albeit one-sided. He just wanted to say *I can hear you,* but he couldn't say anything at all. He would lay there and listen as his hair grew longer. The holidays came and went again with more or less the same amount of fanfare. Jeff remembered nurses and doctors coming in and leaving his room from time to time, sometimes talking really loudly and sometimes tiptoeing around as if they would wake him with one wrong step. If only, he thought.

Everything seemed normal, at least what normal had become, until his wife made a visit for the Fourth of July. Then nobody came for the next couple of weeks and that habit carried on for a while. Finally, at some point where Jeff had lost count, his wife showed up.

"I'm sorry I haven't come to talk to you, I was just having a really hard time to come out and do it. It's been nearly two years now…"

It's okay, Jeff wanted to say, but he couldn't say anything.

"You know I blame myself for everything, right? I know, I know, I probably shouldn't, and if you could you'd be telling me that, but I do, and, I think I always will. I just..." she started to cry again, but this time had come prepared with an entire travel package of tissues.

It's okay to cry, just remember I still love you and I don't blame you at all. That was what Jeff wanted to say, but instead he just lay there, unable to say anything.

"It's just so damn hard now, Jeff. I've lost my best friend, my teammate, my partner, my supporter. How am I supposed to get over that? It's like a part of my life has been ripped out and I'll never be able to get it back."

Don't talk like that, Jeff wanted to say. *You haven't lost me, I'm right here, and I always will be. When I'm better we can make up for all the time we missed.* Jeff just lay there and didn't say anything.

"I guess I just don't know what I'm supposed to do now. If this is all part of my master plan, for whatever reason, there's got to be a next step, I'm just having a hard time seeing what it is. And, for what it's worth, I'm not sure I believe in the whole 'master plan' thing anymore anyway. How can I, like this? Why would my husband be taken away from me just as we're starting a life together? It doesn't make sense." She cried into a tissue before continuing. "Maybe someday it will, but right now I'm feeling a lot of anger, but not at you, Jeff. I love you."

I love you too. Jeff lay there in silence, unable to speak.

"Anyway," she said, choking back tears and emotion. "I need to get going, I need to pick up the kids, I just wanted to stop here by myself. They'll make it out here someday too, I just thought that maybe it was a little too soon for them. I just want you to know that I love you Jeff, and I don't blame you for what happened, but I do miss you. The kids and I think about you every day, and I know they miss you too." She bent down to place something on the ground and in that instant it was like someone turned on a light for Jeff. He was no longer limited to sound only but could see the world around him. Unfortunately, it was not the world he was expecting. He watched as his wife placed a single rose at the base of a gravestone. His vision was now hovering above his wife, staring down at her and the plot of ground where he was buried.

"I love you." His wife turned around and for the first time in over two years Jeff could see her face. She was as beautiful as he remembered and it tore at his heart to see tears streaking down her skin. He wanted to reach out and hold her for the rest of eternity, just cradle her in his arms. He wanted to tell her that everything was okay and that they were okay. Most of all he wanted to tell her that he loved her and didn't blame her and just wanted to be with her.

I love you, Jeff wanted to say, but he couldn't say anything.

GHOSTS

He was awake but he wasn't fully aware of everything around him. His mind was still hazy and he wished he could fall back asleep. He dragged his heavy legs out of the bed and dropped them onto the carpet. He rubbed his eyes for a solid minute and only stopped when the shapes he could see started fleeing the total darkness.

"What happened?" He whispered. He couldn't fully remember the night before, and although it wasn't the first time, he didn't recall having any alcohol to make him forget his night like he was doing right now. He scratched his head and tried to remember anything about the previous evening when he heard a noise in the hall, like someone banging on the wall.

"Hello?" He whipped his head around to see the walkway but it was no use. Everything was drowned out in darkness and he could only make out the faint outline of his doorway. He stared for a few seconds and another bang came from further down the other end. He stood up. Murmurs drifted from the hall to his room and caused him to jump.

"Who's there?" He clenched his fists and started walking toward the noise. "Kaitlin?" He thought (and hoped) his ex-girlfriend had spent the night, but it was a long shot at best. He approached his door and looked out into the hall. His eyes had adjusted but still couldn't see much. A light came on and pots and pans rattled in the kitchen. He grasped the edges of the frame.

"Kaitlin?" He called out louder this time. The noises stopped and for at least a minute he and whoever was in the kitchen were frozen in time, listening, watching and waiting. As the time passed he tried to brace and prepare himself both physically and mentally to engage with whatever was in the kitchen, ex-girlfriend or intruder. He thought he would have scared off a trespasser, but drug addicts were known to not care about the proprietors before, especially in this neighborhood.

He crept down the hallway, trying to pick up any clues he could from the kitchen. Who was invading his property? Why were they here? What were they looking for? How would he get them out? Millions of thoughts were running through his head as he made his way toward the bathroom door. A loud slam came from the kitchen and he ducked into the bathroom. He paused and waited, his heart was running like he had just worked out for an hour. Could it be someone else? What had he done last night?

Just as he was trying to piece everything together he heard a cough come from his bedroom. His heart ran faster. Was there someone in the bed with him and he didn't realize it? The cough got closer and now he could tell someone was walking down the hall. He thought he would be confrontational, but instead he slinked deeper into the bathroom to hide in the shadows. As he waited, sweating now, the person in the hall passed the bathroom door and he could tell that it was a man. What the hell? He couldn't make sense of it anymore, was this all a dream? The most realistic dream he had ever had?

"Sorry, did I wake you?" A woman's voice came from the kitchen, but it didn't sound like Kaitlin.

"No, I was already awake, decided just to get up." A man spoke now, the man from his bedroom. Or was it even his bedroom anymore? He tried to decode the fogginess to remember what happened last night.

"Did you hear noises this morning?" The woman asked.

"You mean besides you?" The man laughed.

"I'm serious," she said. "I thought I heard a voice coming from the hallway. And then it sounded like someone was walking down the hall. At first I thought it was you..."

"Sorry," the man replied. "I didn't hear a thing."

"I know, and you never do, but this isn't the first time either. Remember what I told you about last week? And then the time a month ago?"

A month ago? What happened a month ago? Have they been here for a month? Had he been sleeping next to a stranger that long? Was he in a coma? What was going on? His breathing was frantic, his heart was ready to explode and his face was sweaty. He was desperately trying to unravel this mystery.

"I know dear," the man from the kitchen said. "You think this place is haunted."

"I don't think, I know."

He closed the bathroom door.

"See? Did you hear that?" The woman asked.

He flipped on the lights.

"I did," the man said. "Let me check."

His heart stopped. Or, he thought, it had been stopped all along. He couldn't see his reflection in the mirror. The bathroom walls seemed to collapse in on him and the air became bogged down like a foggy night. His body tingled and he began to shake. He could hear the man coming down the hall, but didn't care anymore. He remembered what happened to him. He hadn't turned on the bathroom lights at all, he had just opened his own eyes.

The bathroom door swung open and the man flipped on the lights only to reveal an empty bathroom. "Nothing here," he called out. "I guess we're both just hearing things."

He stared at the now familiar man in the doorframe. He was in his pajamas, unshaven and tired-looking from too many nights at the office. His wife didn't trust him, he had a bad smoking habit and he kept dark secrets from anyone close to him.

Everything became clear to him and he realized that he remembered all of this because he had been here for months, for years, living in this house and learning all about the people who lived here while trying to figure out why he was here. He knew all of the details about them, and no matter how dark and twisted things got, he was jealous, because at least they were alive.

OTHER WORLDLY

What if I told you that I could show you another world, a magical world? Would you believe me? Would you take me up on the offer? What if I told you that you could already see this world and you look at it every day? You still wouldn't believe me, would you? I can see how you wouldn't, but it's true. The problem is that your memory of this world isn't so good.

When you dream, you're looking into this magical world. Your brain turns into a telescope and focuses in on this other dimension, this other world, and for the most part this world is just like ours. There are people, there are buildings, there are cars, there are trees and plants and rivers and the same basic outline we have on Earth. The big difference is that the laws of nature and the rules of physics as we know them, don't apply there, but don't tell that to the people who live there and know nothing else. They live within these boundaries and they have special mathematical formulas to prove them and they know nothing else. They're used to the weird properties, but your brain isn't, so it gets confused easily when trying to understand this world.

The people look like us, but they're not human. These people can take the shape of anyone, or anything, depending on who's looking at them. The same goes for the buildings, trees and everything else. They all look different depending on who is looking at them, so they're not the same for everybody. They have advanced technology and can detect who is looking in on their world. When a viewer is detected all of the people and objects in this world try and take on the look of something familiar to the person watching. We're not sure why but we think it has something to do with them trying to make their world more comfortable for your overwhelmed brain.

The people in this world live normal lives and go about it whether or not they're being watched by someone, which they are almost all the time. The only thing they really change is their appearance. From time to time they will try to communicate but it never works. They only get through to someone when they scare them (a nightmare for the dreamer) but they've found out that only makes the watcher shy away from their world instead of talking to them. That's not the way they want their world to be perceived and misunderstood, so they don't reach out too often, instead they pretend that no one is watching and live their lives with different faces.

The things they do may seem strange to us, like float around on top of mountains, wrestle sheep in the middle of downtown, hunt for treasure in an abandoned cave, launch space shuttles out of their roofs, climb really tall ladders just to get to a glass of root beer, pave their roads with carpet and have buffalo parades through town or ride around on swans between luxurious hotel rooms, but these strange things are just what happens in their world.

Everything is normal to them, you just don't understand it.

PARALYSIS

Her eyes popped open but she couldn't move. She couldn't even scream. She started panicking. The up-beat rhythm of her heart made her shirt move up and down. She felt a bead of sweat fall down the side of her face, followed shortly by another one. She could feel coolness following her hairline. Her eyes darted back and forth throughout the blacked-out room looking for clues where there were none. She blinked hard and then did it again hoping she would wake up, but she was already awake.

Her body was frozen. She willed her arm, her leg, her waist, anything to move but nothing complied. It was like a bad nightmare where you can't outrun the monster no matter how hard you pump your legs, except this wasn't a nightmare, it was worse. It was like being accidentally locked in a box that you couldn't break out of, except the box was her body and she couldn't break out of it even if she tried hard enough.

At first she thought she was paralyzed. She wasn't sure how that could happen, but maybe she rolled over her neck the wrong way in her sleep. She's been known to flail around before but never thought much about it. She thought it was possible but unlikely.

Her mind jumped to spider myths she had heard so much about. Her eyes danced across the room looking for clues of the whereabouts of a spider capable of paralyzing an adult-sized human. There was a glimmer of moonlight hitting something shiny in a long-forgotten corner and she thought maybe it was a spider web, but she couldn't be sure. She had only ever seen smaller spiders around before, and those were too busy to bother her, running up and down a cobweb in the corner of the garage, doing whatever it is that spiders do. She felt guilty killing them, but apparently they did not feel the same.

That's when the thought hit her, maybe she was dead. Was it possible? Was this what death is like? Was a person forever trapped in their last physical position and geographical location when they died? It was possible, she thought, but also unlikely. She had never heard of any near-death experiences where a person was just stuck in time. She wasn't an expert, but she had heard things.

Her mind was wandering, lost in thoughts that distracted her from her desperate situation. She was on the verge of falling back to sleep, that moment where your mind isn't fully aware of its surroundings but is turned on enough to know something isn't right. Her instincts kicked back in when her brain realized that not only were things not right but they weren't anywhere near being right, especially now that the walls were melting.

Like a spilled bottle of syrup, the walls were running down the house, unable to stop once they reached the floor. Soon after the walls began their dance the ceiling started melting in on itself, and it looked like she was underneath a giant funnel. Her panic set in again. Was she having a bad trip? She didn't remember taking anything. The melting walls snapped back into place and she could hear voices now but couldn't see what they belonged to. The ceiling opened up and a creature with the head of a lizard peeked in her roof and watched her from above. He flipped his tongue out, but it never went back in his mouth. The lizard tongue swirled through the room and wrapped around the mirror against the dresser and landed on the foot rest of her bed.

Her panic kicked into high gear.

She wanted to move, she wanted to run away but the mysterious restraints kicked in and gripped with a relentless hold. All she could do was stare at her lifeless limbs and exert everything her mind knew about moving muscles. She was focused so hard that she felt like she could accomplish anything. Any test she had ever taken, any intense situation she had been involved with felt like a breeze compared to staring down her arm and wanting it to move so badly. The ceiling lizard produced a treacherous claw and reached in and landed on top of her body. She was pinned down, not any longer by a mysterious force but instead by a scaly, three-pronged talon.

The tears started pooling around her neck and indicated that they were not paralyzed. Her entire neck and up seemed okay. She could blink, wiggle her ears, clear her throat and twitch her nose, but none of those things could help her move around or otherwise survive. She knew something was wrong and in order to keep living she'd have to overcome it, but she didn't know if it was something she could overcome. It seemed to be a supernatural force demonstrating its power and after what seemed like days passing by she knew it was more powerful than her. The force kept producing hallucinations and all she could do was sit back, cry and wait for it to be over.

The red digits on the digital clock beside her glowed against her face and she could move her eyes far enough to see that 30 minutes had passed. They had been 30 minutes of nothing but agony and torture. It was the worst half hour in her memory banks. She could no longer comprehend how actual torture could be any worse but she had a deeper understanding of the pain endured during.

After an hour of screaming, yelling and being a statue stuck underneath a five-pound blanket, among other things, she gave up hope. After two hours she started hoping for the worst. She was hoping that lizard would come back and squash her to death. At least then she wouldn't have to experience this again. After hour number three she started to lose track of the hours, they seemed to roll by and disappear as quickly as her hope. She started to accept her new lifestyle and her mind kept drifting to what it would be like to exist in this state forever. It wasn't something she wanted for herself, but after hours of spending your life not being able to move, certain things are accepted and assumptions about normal life are thrown out the window. She was at a point where she just didn't care.

The time kept slipping away, but she didn't notice until her alarm clock went off. It caught her off guard, just like every morning, no matter how many times she had been woken up by it. She reached her hand up and out of the covers and hit the snooze button. She put her hand back by her side and rolled over. Seconds later she sprang to life and waved her hands in front of her face. Was it all a dream? It felt realistic enough, but she didn't have to worry anymore.

It was over, she realized. It was over at last.

FROM UNDER THE BED

Yes, monsters are hiding in your closet.

They're under your bed, too.

They're also behind your door, under your desk, inside your drawer, above your ceiling fan and just around the corner. The monsters are in another dimension, so they can be almost anywhere they want. They can only appear in our dimension wherever they won't get stuck or break anything. It's hard to appear in the middle of a wall, for example.

The monsters aren't bad, they just have a bad reputation. First, they don't look anything like humans, so that's a big obstacle to begin with. We're talking scales, fur, multiple eyes, one eye, blue skin, green skin, claws, hooves, hunchbacks and lanky limbs. Sometimes the disadvantage of having two heads can't be overcome. Secondly, Hollywood hasn't helped at all even though they have gotten a lot right. Halloween doesn't help either. It's the first time for a lot of kids to be exposed to scary and creepy monsters. You never really see helpful or caring monsters.

All the monsters really want to do is study humans. They're curious. It's just like humans studying insects, except scarier. It's the reason the monsters don't come out in the middle of the day, it would just make their lives more challenging. Can you imagine the chaos if a monster appeared out of nowhere in the middle of downtown Chicago? Or in the bottom of the seventh at the World Series? The few times someone tried it, they were mistaken for Bigfoot, a Yeti or the Loch Ness monster. "Thanks Brent," all the monsters say when they see each other. Brent feels bad about it. He even cut his hair short and died it red, but everybody still remembers.

So to avoid all potential problems, the monsters only come out at night. And since their main goal is to study humans, they go where the humans are; the bedroom. It's not really their fault that kids are light sleepers, it's just kind of the way it is. When a kid senses one of them and wakes up, the monster has to head out of there as fast as he can. Luckily for the monsters, inter-dimensional travel happens instantly. While there are stories out there about monsters appearing out from underneath the bed or inside a closet, the two most common locations in the monster world, nobody has any proof, and that's all the monsters really care about.

When they're past the stage of worrying about getting caught, they study the humans sleep. They get up really close and examine the faces, and they awe at how each one is different, no matter how many times they do the study. They evaluate breathing patterns and sleeping positions and even objects in the room. The monsters all meet afterwards to map out any conclusions, interesting finds and outstanding questions.

The monsters are fascinated by socks, too, most likely because they have no feet, they just float around places. Did I forget to mention that earlier? Because of this fascination, they steal socks to be able to study them more in-depth. So while your laundry machines take the blame, it's the monsters you should be worried about.

The monsters have sketches of people. Tall people, short people, fat people, skinny people and they make different combinations of each, and they're still amazed that there are more combinations than they can come up with. They make figurines of humans they have seen, complete with wardrobe and socks, and they study those when they aren't able to transport themselves into our dimension.

The biggest mystery to the monsters is how humans communicate. At first they all thought it was some kind of snoring and grunting language that we had developed, but they soon realized that the humans did have words. However, most of the time what they heard was yelling, so they assumed all the words to be loud and high-pitched. So they practice their human voices and human calls and even put on plays about humans with very loud dialog.

You might be asking yourself why the monsters go to all this trouble. It's the first question that most people ask, and really the answer is simple. It's because they want to be like us. They want to be accepted. All they know is rejection, so the monsters study and examine and research how to be human, just to keep their hope alive that someday they can be part of the human race.

Rendering Sleep Meaningless

We all thought it would be a good idea.

We all said we wanted it and would pay dearly for it.

We ended up making the biggest mistake we could have ever made.

At first, when there were rumors of a pill that could make your body capable of bypassing sleep, everyone was a bit skeptical. Who wouldn't be? Sleep had been essential for as long as anyone had been around. Who was this company claiming everyone who had ever lived wasted countless hours lying horizontally on a soft surface?

The claims were quickly and fiercely backed up by studies, research grants, numerous experiments and volunteers and witnesses from all over the globe. Their product was legitimate and very much in demand.

The usage spread as you would imagine any highly sought-after product would. First only the wealthy could afford it and they used it to stay awake and make even more money. They were quick to turn around and use it within their company ranks, ramping up production and they started to see the money pile higher. Over time this brought the cost of the product down significantly and it was opened up to a brand-new audience.

It wasn't long before these pills were as prevalent as a caramel latte. Everyone who ever wanted an extra eight hours in the day was taking them, which covered about nine out of every nine people. Some used it to be extra productive and work longer hours for a promotion or take on another job, while some others pursued hobbies they never had time for when sleep got in the way.

It all worked really well for a while, and we all liked it, but then the real world got in the way. Companies lobbied to have 60-hour work weeks become the standard with 70-hour weeks soon to follow. We all groaned and knew 80-hour weeks were coming, but there wasn't much we could do about it.

Lots of industries died simply because they weren't needed any more. If a company sold beds, they no longer sold anything. Bed and breakfasts turned into just more locally-owned restaurants and hotels became glorified storage lockers. The real estate industry had a drastic shift to match a similar one in construction. Bedrooms were no longer "in." Instead we all started adding extra game rooms, exercise rooms and unnecessary offices. A lot of people didn't build any extra rooms and a lot of houses were downsized or built smaller, which cut into the profit of home builders. The only industry to grow was the food industry. The lack of sleep even spawned a new meal in what used to be the middle of the night. However, because of this, everyone got a little bit fatter and the health of the nation took a nosedive when we thought it had already bottomed out.

Dying industries caused unemployment to jump. Then companies started replacing two workers with one, then three to one and some moved on to four to one which caused the ranks of the unemployed to spike above 50 percent. The government tried to help, but unemployment benefits and social security only lasted so long. Crime rose just because people were trying to survive and everyone started watching their backs 24 hours a day.

This all accumulated with us walking around paranoid for our well-being and instead of our free time increasing like we all thought, we just spent more hours at the office, which was hardly a benefit. Everything became more stressful than it had ever been.

The stress didn't subside when we found out there was no going back. Our bodies adjusted and even if we stopped taking the pill we would never sleep again. Just knowing what it used to be like and not realizing we'd ever experience it again made the suicide rate jump off its own ledge. The average lifespan dropped by 20 years and we were helpless to avoid it.

We were all depressed and outraged that we hadn't known this ahead of time. We tried to reverse the course but it was too late for most of us. We had to instill in our children the importance of sleep and what it used to mean to us.

We thought we had it all figured out, but we were all wrong.

NAPS

Naps are nature's energy boost.

Caffeine? Not needed.
Sugar? Unnecessary.
Guarana? See caffeine.

Napping is what made humans what they are today. Why do you think babies nap so much? It's so they can store up the energy to keep the developmental process running strong. If they didn't nap their energy would be so low that their growth would be stunted and it would take them longer to learn new concepts.

Napping provides energy.

Warriors used to nap before all of their biggest fights. It's hard to imagine overly-macho men who would regularly battle to the death in bare feet and little protection taking a nap on a bed of straw and hay, but that's what would happen. Before they could run around and be the strong warriors they were portrayed as they had to have the energy stored to keep the image up.

When an army is protecting their barracks overnight in the middle of enemy territory the only way they stay alert is to nap. One person guards for an hour while the other guard naps. When the nap is over, the guards change places and the first guard starts his nap. These naps provide the guardsmen with the energy they need to protect the rest of their unit from the enemy just beyond the hill.

In survival mode a person kicks into nap mode. When you're hiking around and lost in the forest one of the best ways to get out of the situation is to take a quick nap before heading onward. This way you don't have to stop for one big chunk of time in the middle of the night. You can keep plowing your way through the trees faster and hope that you find a way out with enough energy leftover to use if a desperate situation arises and you have to get yourself out of a jam.

Numerous studies have revealed what should have already been obvious to us all. Napping intermediately throughout the day helps to improve our performance in tasks, increase our mental capacity and feel better and be happier overall. That's why they tell you to take a break to rest in between strenuous activities and sleep in the middle of a work day. Next time your boss catches you with your eyes closed at your desk just say that you want to make sure you're fully prepared for the afternoon meeting.

Napping is essential and there's no way around it. It's almost as much of a requirement for us as food or air or water. Nobody wants to acknowledge it because there's been a social stigma on it for quite some time. People view naps as a weakness now instead of as a way to build strengths. People view naps as being lazy and not wanting to contribute or get anything done. People view naps as a cop-out to the stresses of modern-day life. People have all of these negative views on naps but the last time they napped was before they knew the whole alphabet.

If people tried it more they might just end up enjoying it and realizing it has benefits that used to be obvious to everyone.

RAIN

He was distracted and couldn't sleep. The heavy raindrops made thumps as they landed against his window. He was used to them now and used them as staccato points to a melody running through his head. When the lightning flashed in the window it was a cymbal exploding in the rear of the room and when the thunder followed it was a timpani roll to bring the musicians to the next stanza. He composed masterpieces from underneath his covers, trying to fall asleep while a violent rage tested the trees outside his room.

In his head the audience loved every crescendo, every tempo change and every flail of his arms. He was front and center, waving his hands to guide the orchestra at every note on the page. He imagined his hair flapping to the rhythm of the beat and the coattails of his tuxedo swaying back and forth in a similar fashion. For the finale he picked up the excitement and fury and the chamber matched the anger of the storm outside. With a final, animated swish of his arms he spun in place to face the audience, who was now standing and cheering, and took several bows. The musicians followed and their praise continued until the next thunder boom shook the house.

He was jarred out of his imagination and thrown back in his bed. He hadn't been dreaming but it had felt like one of the best dreams he had ever had. No matter, he thought, he would just recreate it. He laid his head back on his pillow and listened to the splashing landing patterns of the rain.

When the rain threw itself against the siding of the house it carried the sound of a hollow thud, like a fist against an empty section of wall. He expanded on the sound and imagined a thousand carpenters hammering nails into wood. He was too close to the construction to see what they were building so he took a step back, and then another, and then a couple more until he was finally far enough away to get the entire vision in his head. The rain didn't cease so the hammering carried on at full pace.

Little slivers of silver were flying back and forth as the men hammered the wood in place and moved on to their next target. They had the system down as there wasn't a break in the tap-tap pattern when one man moved into his next position. From far away he watched the men work resiliently and with every minute that passed the immense log cabin they were building became more real, clearer and sharper. Men moved onto the roof, still without missing a beat. Scaffolding was assembled and disassembled as quickly as the walls could be built to support it. They were the fastest carpenters he had ever seen and they worked in silence except for their hammers which were continually pounding away.

Outside his bedroom window a flash of lightning zipped across the sky followed closely by a thunder boom. Inside his mind one of the men had knocked a box of nails off the roof and it had landed, ricocheted and bounced on, around and through the scaffolding. When this happened, none of the men stopped working and, in fact, had seemed to increase the speed of their striking hammers.

He walked closer to the increasingly finished building and found his way to the front door. There were no carpenters here; they had all moved around to the back of the building trying to finish it as fast as they could. He reached for the handle of the large, oak door and turned. It swung open with surprising ease and he was facing a cavernous room that smelled like pine. He could hear the noise of the hammers bouncing off the walls toward the back of the room and took one step closer.

Another thunder clap shook the house and the monstrous wooden lodge disintegrated into his bedroom where there were no carpenters but only raindrops again. He tossed and turned until he found a cozy spot within his bed and again focused on the rain being whipped around outside. The storm had only gotten stronger and the rain was more intense.

As the rain fell on the roof he imagined machine guns pelting bullets against metal and when he opened his mind further the metal disappeared and he was thrust into a warzone. He was an observer, not a participant, and from his vantage point up high on a balcony he could see a street below lined with armies from both sides. They were engaged in combat, exchanging bullets with one another but something was off. He looked down below and could see smoke billowing from the gun barrels, and he could see bullets bouncing around off the ground and surrounding buildings, but he never saw any of the soldiers hit. They were standing about 50 feet apart, firing every bullet they had, but couldn't hit anything but the crumbling buildings and the dirt road.

The magazines were endless and the soldiers never had to reload. They braced themselves against whatever they had and fired at will. There were no leaders, there were no rules and chaos ruled below the 30-foot high balcony he was leaning over. The sky was gray and the rest of the town seemed abandoned. No one noticed him up high and he imagined he was the puppeteer for every marionette soldier below. When he thought about a soldier shooting out a window, the soldier did. When he imagined a soldier kneeling, the soldier did. He realized he had full control over this seemingly chaotic scene and he felt like a god.

The town wasn't familiar, the uniforms weren't like anything he had seen and the only constant was the buzzing of the bullets and the thud-like sounds coming from their impact against anything but the other soldiers. Even if he tried to make one soldier aim for another, the soldier would miss. Instead the bullet would whizz by the other soldier's ear and smash into the unsuspecting doorframe of the local post office.

When the lightning struck outside, in his imagination another pane of glass was shattered by misfired munitions. When the thunder rolled through it was another tank rumbling onto the battlefield with backups for the poorly-trained soldiers. At one point he counted 300 men to each side, crammed in the narrow street of this tiny town and still not managing to hit anyone or be hit by anyone else. It was the sight of an oddly uniform chaos magnified by the increasing noise of missing bullets.

The wind howled outside and it was time for a new position. He rolled onto his back and stared at the ceiling. The storm was raging on and the rain was now coming in sideways. He closed his eyes and listened to the beats in the distance. In his head he imagined they were tap shoes at a concert. At first the concert was small, just a man and a woman dancing side-by-side. They were elegant and graceful and never missed a beat. They were in-step with one another, moving from stage-right to stage-left in an impressive show of tap.

The two were joined by another couple and the music didn't slow down. Props and sets were brought on stage and the men flung the women back and forth and between pillars and on top of tables until they were joined by more people. The group of tap dancers was spread out now and flailing their legs around like popped balloons trying to escape. They jumped from high places to low places and back again without a single dancer out of step.

There was no audience that he could see and it was oddly quiet except for the metal-tipped shoes. They clanged and clacked against a boring stage and echoed throughout the room. The feverish dancers were dripping with sweat but couldn't slow down, it was like someone was forcing them to dance faster than they ever thought possible. The pace picked up and the rhythm of the tapping quickened to an unknown song.

He jolted straight up in his bed only to find that the storm outside had ended and was replaced by rays of sunlight. He ran to his window to see the evidence of the storm. When he glanced out the window and looked around he was stunned to see no trail left behind. The concrete wasn't wet, the trees looked healthy and the grass was as dry as it had been during the drought. He walked back over to his bed and sat at the edge. The images of orchestral masterpieces, luxurious log cabins, mismanaged warriors and fervent dancers flashed in his mind.

He wondered if he dreamt the whole thing.

JOURNAL

Day 1

So far so good. 24 hours without sleep isn't as bad as I thought it would be, of course, that's what everyone says. I've kept myself entertained with videogames, movies and lots and lots of mindless TV. I'm updated on all of the latest infomercials though, so if you have a question about the "Roller Ab Power Max" machine, I can recite all the lines from that ad. Moving into hour 25 and I'm feeling good. Lots of coffee, lots of soda, lots of everything because there's so much time.

Day 2

My productivity has crashed. After the first day I felt strong and was getting a lot done, but now I'm coming down from wherever that push came from. I'm pretty tired and have kept the watchers busy keeping me awake. They seem to have some sort of surround sound system installed here and I can confirm the "Volume Up" button works. I'm finding that I have forgotten some things that I only later remembered having done before. For example, I watched the same episode of *COPS* within just two hours of one another, and I didn't realize it until the episode was half over. Either way, I'm starting to feel the effects and am missing my warm bed. They said it wouldn't be easy and they weren't lying.

Physically I feel worse than expected. I anticipated the worst part of this to be mental, but sitting here now I can tell it's taken a toll all over. I'm starting to shake and feel light-headed. I'm sure the watchers won't let anything terrible happen to me, but still I have a terrible feeling about this and am starting to have doubts.

Day 3

Bed. Sleep. Pillows. It's all I can think about. It's a struggle to eat sometimes because I fall asleep in the middle of a meal. My meals are regular but I'm having a hard time eating them. I know they're watching me. They should help me instead of blasting noises. I'm sure they have a surround sound system installed and it must be a good one. All the TV shows have become boring and I can't find anything to enjoy. Enjoy. Enjoy. I'm so bored and I just want to sleep. I'm still shaking all the time. I don't feel well.

Day 4

I can hardly stand, I have to sit all the time. My mind and body is in pain. I'm no longer hungry either. I think the TV burns my eyes.

Day 5

Someone should have helped by noww. Thisi sn't fun.

Day 6

? PLEASE end this. I feel like Death.

Day 7

HELP mE I KNOW YOU CAN READ THIS. EXPERIMENT IS OVER

Day 8

<illegible>

Day 9

The smell. It's the smell. It reminds
Me
    Of   home. something
Familiar. Ive been locked in this sell for 11 days,

its gotta be 11 days. The darkness is madening. IT's all dark.
All gray. The pills.

Kills pills is what I hear. Kils pills. And pain. The
Christmas song about mice stirring? They're stirring in the
walls. Clawing, trying to get in. The watchers are *<illegible>*
but I know what they
Really want.
I know they reall want.

I can't tho, I can't tel
L
Wy? if I were there I would help. Ican't feel any thing.
<illegible>

Day 10
<illegible>

Day 11

No entry

WHAT IT MEANS

To a baby, sleep means having time to grow and develop. Every time a baby wakes up, they're a little bigger, a little smarter and a little more aware of their surroundings. It's also the way they spend most of their lives and what they know the best. It's cozy, warm, comfortable and familiar for them. It's nice for them and relaxing, a way to escape from a crazy world where everything is much larger than they are and nothing makes sense.

A child views sleep as an inconvenience. It's a time when they are dragged away from their fun and games while all the "adults" get to stay up and have more fun. It's a time when they'll constantly ask for "Just five more minutes," hoping that their mom or dad forgets and they can actually sneak in 15 or 30 to construct their building block town or color another page in their book or set up and protect their fort in the basement. They don't realize how important sleep is for them and they don't care.

For a teenager, sleep is a double-edged sword. They fight it all night long, drinking caffeine and stimulating their senses in front of electronics to try and beat the ever-increasing yawns and grogginess that they feel. They push their parents for extended curfews and even then tend to break them more often than not. After all these hours of staying awake and talking to all their friends and avoiding homework at all costs, they'll finally throw in the towel and jump into bed in the early hours of the morning. Then, when seven in the morning comes and they have to get up and get ready for school, trying to get them up is more challenging than running a half-marathon. They hide under the covers, break their alarm clocks, kick and scream until there are five minutes left until school starts. They fight the urge to wake up as much as they fight the urge to fall asleep in the first place. When night falls again, the cycle starts all over.

In college sleep is more of an annoyance than anything. Regarding sleep, everyone acts like a teenager without any outside influences like parents telling them when to go to bed and wake up. Sometimes sleep is avoided all together and the night is spent studying for an exam in the morning. Other times sleep is avoided just to stay up and drink late into the night. When a college-aged person does sleep though, they don't mess around and sometimes sleeping in as late as noon is considered getting up early. A lot of people sleep through classes whether or not they're in the classroom or at home. There is no normal sleep pattern and everyone recognizes this, but nobody finds it weird.

Once a person is married sleep becomes a routine. After a while of having a stable job and a spouse the sleep schedule balances out and after a long enough time the schedule is predictable and comfortable. For a lot of people this can be the first stage where sleep is actually desired instead of forced upon them by some outside factor. It's nice and relaxing and comfortable again. A person is reminded how much they need sleep and how important it is and they take advantage of it as much as they can.

Having a kid changes everything. It's like starting a new life. You have the same name, you live in the same house and you have the same job, but everything is different. Sleep is an unobtainable goal and you are well aware of just how far-fetched it is, like winning the lottery or ever having six more zeroes on the end of your bank account balance. Sleep eludes you at every turn, mocking you as if to say "I know you want to sleep and take care of yourself, but I know you can't. You're not number one anymore." You stand in the living room, rocking your baby back and forth trying to get them to fall asleep all the while thinking you're going to pass out, fall over and injure both of you. You're jealous of your spouse sleeping in your room, but you know that an hour from now your roles will be reversed and that's when you realize that you will get sleep and that it will come but it might not be soon enough. Even when you do have a chance to get some rest, it won't be for very long and before you know it you'll be awake again and expected to perform well at your job and take care of your child. It's almost like you're torturing yourself, but when you look down at your baby nestled in your arms, you wouldn't have it any other way.

When a person has kids they become a director of sleep rather than a consumer. They manage schedules with their own and define strict rules and stick to them. With kids, bedtimes are set in stone and they know it. With teenagers, curfews are enforced down to the minute and a parent is up and waiting 30 minutes afterwards to dole out punishments. It's not easy, but it has to be done. The parents try to mesh schedules with their own but in the end, the only thing they know for sure is that they'll be the last ones to lie down and the first ones to get up. This will continue until all of their children are out of the house, so they're in it for the long haul and they get settled in.

When all the children are out of the house, a couple has a hard time getting back to where they used to be. All they've known for the longest time is taking care of children in the house, and without kids around anymore, they have to get to know each other again. Sleep at this phase takes some adjustment, but once they get settled down and get their schedules straight, it's a lot like when they were first married. The difference here is they find themselves even more tired than they remembered since they finally have time to realize what their bodies are telling them. This pushes bedtimes earlier and earlier and sleep is once again at the front of their concerns. It's relaxing and nice and well-deserved.

After retirement, sleep is like icing on a cake. A person's responsibility has changed and is now solely focused on themselves. They still host family functions and babysit the grandkids from time to time, but normal everyday life is like sleep used to be for them; relaxing, comfortable, nice and definitely needed. When it's time to go to bed, it's as if their body is telling them that they don't have to, but they probably should. They aren't necessarily tired, but at this point in their life it's what's supposed to happen around this time of the day, so they crawl into bed and think about how their time is going to be occupied tomorrow.

The last stage of thinking about sleep is also the worst. After their grandkids are grown and starting to have their own kids, a person views sleep mostly as what their life is. They wake up for a while, maybe doze off or take a nap while watching TV, eat dinner and then go to bed early since there's nothing else to do. It gets worse and worse over time and eventually sleep is viewed as entering the unknowable abyss. There's always that possibility in a person's mind that they will never wake up. They lie down and wonder if this is the day. At the very end, sometimes a person is wishing it to be so.

Sleep is a constant throughout a person's life. Sometimes the way a person views it is happy and positive, while other times it can be an annoyance or even negative and depressing. It's one thing we can all relate to no matter our background or our age. It gives strength and growth and hope and can influence our thinking. No matter what it means to you, there's no denying that it's a powerful tool.

SLEEPOVER

"What do you want to watch now?" Lindsay asked Mackenzie who was grasping for the last kernel of popcorn in the bowl.

"Doesn't this have a sequel?" Mackenzie threw the last piece into her mouth.

"Oh yeah, let's watch that."

"Do you want more popcorn?" Mackenzie asked.

"Well we'll need some now that you've eaten it all, right?" Lindsay made a face.

"I'll get it." Mackenzie returned the look with her own stupid one.

"I'll set up the movie." Lindsay walked over to the shelf that housed all the movies. Since Mackenzie's parents didn't keep them in any order she threw the first scary movie into the first empty slot and started scanning for its sequel.

Mackenzie ascended the boxy stairwell up to the darkened living room. When she reached the carpeted floor of the living area she looked further up the stairs and saw the glow from her parent's bedroom creep its way down the hall. They had probably dozed off in front of the late night show so she didn't worry about making too much noise. She walked to the kitchen and reached for the shelf above the spices, where all of the buttery goodness of microwave popcorn was stored. She set the bowl down on the counter and reached for the second-to-last bag in the box. She ripped off the plastic wrapping, threw it in the microwave and hit the pre-programmed button.

Mackenzie leaned against the counter and tapped her finger against the dark granite as the kernels began to pop one at a time. She stared out the window above the sink toward the empty field that her father spent most of his time avoiding household chores in. There was an old barn out there, barely outlined against the night sky. She remembered being out there many times as a kid, but didn't have much reason to go out there anymore. Her father kept all of his tools out there as well as the bigger equipment that wouldn't fit in their three-car garage.

The kernels were picking up speed, popping faster and rattling against the side of the package. Mackenzie did a quick glance at the clock to see that there were still 30 seconds left, so she turned her eyes to the distant barn again. In a split second, she thought she saw the barn door open and close. She blinked and looked again, but nothing moved. Maybe it was a trick of the mind, she thought. Maybe the noise of the popcorn confused her senses and she saw something that wasn't there.

The microwave dinged and Mackenzie jumped. Her heart was racing, but she reminded herself that her parents were upstairs and her best friend was waiting downstairs. She grabbed the steaming bag from the microwave, dumped it all into the bowl and walked a little faster down the stairs.

"Hey, what took so long?" Lindsay asked before Mackenzie came into eyesight.

"I just freaked myself out, no big deal."

"It's just popcorn, Kenzy."

"I know. Shut up. What are you doing?" She walked in the room and noticed the television was paused at the opening credits for the next scary movie.

"Just waiting for you." She looked up from her phone. "And texting Brandon."

"Brandon, huh? What's he doing tonight?" Mackenzie set the bowl down on the end table.

"Nothing." Lindsay went back to furiously hammering out half-complete sentences on her phone.

"Bullshit. Did you guys end up hooking up last night?" Mackenzie knew the answer, she had heard it today in third period from one of Brandon's friends, but she wanted to hear it from Lindsay.

"Of course, duh."

"You guys are always sneaking off to do stuff like that."

"Sorry that some of us have boyfriends. Oh sorry, I guess Tyler is a what? Kinda-boyfriend?"

"He's just..." Mackenzie paused and looked toward the ceiling, "I don't know, you know?"

Before Lindsay could answer a thud came from the floor above them. Both girls jumped and Mackenzie almost sent the popcorn across the room.

"What was that?" Mackenzie looked at Lindsay, who was wide-eyed and didn't seem to have an explanation either. She started heading for the stairs and Lindsay jumped up to follow her.

"Wait…" She was going to continue, but there was nothing else to say. Mackenzie was already at the base of the stairs and stopped for her friend to catch up. Lindsay got there and held onto her friend's hand; they ascended the stairs that way until they reached the living room. Mackenzie looked out from the stairs and glanced upward toward her parent's bedroom. The glow that was there minutes ago no longer existed. She looked around to see if anything was out of place, but didn't notice anything.

"You think it was your parents… you know?" Lindsay chuckled and poked Mackenzie.

"Shut up. It was probably nothing."

"Yeah, right. Come on, I want to watch that movie."

"All right." Mackenzie scanned the house again and her heart pace slowed. They walked back down the stairs.

"So you don't think Tyler and you are going to do anything?"

"We'll mess around, but I'll probably dump him after homecoming, you know?"

"I don't know Kenzy, he's pretty hot."

"I guess, he's just not a good kisser, too much tongue. It's kinda gross."

The girls reached the bottom of the stairs and turned into the media room. Mackenzie saw that the television was now just a black screen.

"Did you turn off the TV?"

"No…" Lindsay spun around and caught her friend's eye. "Was there a power outage or something? Maybe that's what we heard?"

Mackenzie reached for the nearest light switch and flicked it to the on position; the lights were dim but they were illuminated nonetheless. She ran up to the TV and pushed the power button and was greeted by a screen of static. She opened the DVD player.

"There's nothing in here Linds."

"What?" Lindsay half-jogged to her friend to verify she wasn't crazy. "I swear I put it in there."

"I know, I saw the screen."

"What the hell?"

Both girls were startled by a sound from the window at the end of the hallway. It sounded like a giant bird had smashed into it. They both screamed and reached out for one another. Mackenzie grabbed Lindsay's hand and made a dash for her room near the end of the hall in the basement. Her heart was going faster than she ever remembered and Lindsay's wasn't far behind. They got to Mackenzie's room, slammed the door shut and locked it. They both jumped for the bed.

"What's going on Kenzy?"

"I don't know, I don't know." They both hid behind pillows and stared at the door. After moments of sitting in anticipation, Mackenzie broke the silence. "When I was popping popcorn, I think I saw the barn door out back open."

"What?" Lindsay's head swiveled.

"Remember how I said I scared myself? Yeah, I didn't think that was anything, but now I'm not sure anymore."

"Shit Kenzy, why didn't you tell me?"

"I didn't want you to freak out."

"A little late for that now, huh?"

There was a bang at the door and both girls screamed and grabbed their pillows tight enough to almost break their knuckles.

"Maybe it's just Brandon." Mackenzie said through struggled breathe.

"Or Tyler."

Another bang from the door incited the same reaction from the girls.

"How good is that lock?" Lindsay breathed into the pillow.

"I don't know."

There was another bang. Mackenzie picked up her alarm clock, cocked it back and was ready to throw it at whatever was about to come through that door. Lindsay grabbed a stuffed animal from the edge of the bed. A fourth bang broke the lock and the door handle began to turn. The girls screamed.

The door creaked open, inch by inch, until there was enough room for a head to fit through, then it stopped. Both girls sat on the bed, armed with useless weapons and covered in impractical armor. After the longest three seconds of their lives, a head appeared from the open door and it wasn't one that either girl recognized. They unloaded their weapons and Mackenzie screamed the loudest.

Brain's Perspective

Damn that looks comfortable. Weren't we just here? This day went by quick.

Top drawer, pull it open.

Take out that gray shirt, that one's nice and soft. Set it on top.

Pull your shirt over your head. Toss it in the hamper.

Keep breathing.

Gray shirt over the head now.

Remove your pants. Toss them in the hamper.

Walk back over to the door.

Rub your eyes.

Take a quick look around the room. Memorize it.

Turn off the lights.

Keep breathing.

Turn.

Move forward, but be careful, the edge of the bed is about four feet in front of you.

Reach out and feel around with your hands. That's the dresser.

Shuffle your feet against the carpet. Remember the bedposts, don't stub your toe.

Turn again. A few more feet until the night stand.

Okay, we're there. Stop walking.

Feel out for the sheets. There they are, pull them down a bit.

Keep breathing.

Sit at the edge of the bed.

Stretch your arms. Arch your back. That crack was a good one! That feels good.

Swing your feet under the sheets.

It's a bit cold under here. Pull up the sheets quickly.

Yawn.

Lay your head on the pillow.

Pull the sheets up to your chin. It'll warm up soon.

This is comfortable. Scratch your arm. Now it's more comfortable.

I wish we could do this all the time. We deserve this after a long day.

Try to relax.

Think of something totally irrelevant from your past.

Keep breathing.

Try to fall asleep.

NMDD

When you're asleep people visit your house all the time. Even if the doors are locked, the windows are shut and the chimney flue is closed these people will find their way inside your house. They're not burglars, thieves, Santa Claus or anyone looking for trouble, they're just doing their job. It's not a glamorous job, but it has to be done, that's just how it works. They didn't particularly want the job either, but when the economy is down, jobs for microscopic beings are hard to come by.

The most well-known of these beings is the tooth fairy. The actual job position is called "Tooth Collection Engineer." The humans caught a rumor of this being and ran with the idea of a fairy with wings and other nonsense. "Tooth Collectors," what they call themselves, have a hard time shaking that image. They always wear their standard-issued all-white jumpsuit and the profession is split between about 55 percent men and 45 percent women. The men really dislike the tooth fairy misnomer, but they live with it because the pay is good and the job is easy compared to all the other microscopic being jobs they could be doing instead.

Another job performed by one of your nighttime intruders is to give you bad breath. This, by almost everyone's account, is the worst job of the lot. "Halitosis Applicators" (HA's) drag around canisters of spray all night and are forced to climb in and out of a person's mouth to apply it. To coat a human being's mouth takes approximately 30 minutes, and while applying the spray the "HA" has to endure pitch darkness, damp conditions, loud snoring vibrations and has to avoid the tongue the entire time. There's no easy way to do that, but their training can sometimes be months-long just to make them agile and aware enough to be able to do their job safely. This position has the highest turnover rate as well as the highest fatality rate and the highest workplace injury rate. This position is always open but always difficult to fill.

"Gound Engineers" are the people that make sure you have plenty of gound, or eye goop, in your eyes when you wake up. The job is pretty straight forward and just requires the worker to pack the substance in the corner of your eye as tight as they can and make sure it doesn't come dislodged during a normal sleep pattern. The difficult part of the job is dragging the gound around all evening. It's a heavy, dense mixture made up of dust, mucus and blood and skin cells. It smells terrible and it follows a Gound Engineer all night, even after their work shift is over, like working in a restaurant that uses garlic in every dish.

There are little beings running around your pillow all night in charge of making sure your hair is nice and oily and messy in the morning and they're called "Disheveled Stylists."

The job isn't glamorous, but a lot of them went to school to be able to learn the right combinations of oils to get your hair looking just wrong enough to not be able to walk out the door first thing after waking up. Their tricky combination of oils gets all over the place, including your pillow, your face and sometimes your sheets, but these stylists think it just adds to their creative genius and they continue to make you look worse and worse throughout the night.

"Oxygen Deprivation Specialists" cause you to yawn, but their work starts before you're asleep and continues after you wake. They're there to make sure you fall asleep and that everyone else is able to do their job, so it's pretty important. Unlike the Gound Engineers and the Halitosis Applicators, they carry around empty tanks all night and slowly fill them up with the oxygen around you, so that you get less and their tanks get full. For some special cases, or especially challenging clients, they have extra-large tanks and spare compartments just in case it takes a while for a person to feel the effects.

"Muscle Reflexologists" (MR's) are the slackers of the group. They come in from time to time, whenever they feel like it really, and play with the muscles in your leg and make you kick yourself awake wildly in the middle of a fantastic dream. Nobody likes them. When you're awake, nobody else can do their job, and when a Muscle Reflexologist enters the room, everyone else knows they have to put all their work on hold until he or she is finished. Luckily for everyone, most MR's do one thing and then leave, just because they're so lazy and don't really want to do any work. Most MR's are still living off of their parents or a large inheritance so they don't do it for the money, just more to be a jerk.

"Organ Control Technologists" (OCT's) is a fancy way to say people who aggravate your body while you sleep. These people are like MR's but even more hated, if that's possible. That cough in the middle of the night? An OCT was kicking your lung. Have to pee at two in the morning? An OCT was jumping on your bladder. OCT's and MR's tend to get in fights a lot because the line between their jobs is so fuzzy, but since MR's are not motivated, the OCT's usually win, so they make more money, are more aggressive and tend to be the bullies of the microscopic community.

"Environment Distortionists" are the lowest entry point on the job ladder at the company. Over 80% of the current workers were an "EnviroDist" at one point or another. Being an EnviroDist is the simplest way to get up to speed on the workings of everyone else. Anyone who is an EnviroDist is usually paired with someone else for the evening. They follow along in their footsteps and watch them perform their work from afar. The only duty that the EnviroDist has is to make subtle changes to the environment that the sleeping human is used to. For example, one of the most popular tactics with EnviroDists is to un-tuck the sheets just enough to make sure they become entirely removed from their position while the human moves around. Another one is to change the alarm clock from AM to PM just to frustrate their subjects. The small changes become bigger over time until it's time for the EnviroDist to move onto another position with more responsibilities.

All of these positions are within the National Microscopic Dormancy Department which is one of the longest-running divisions in the microscopic community. They provide lots of good-paying jobs and have a very healthy budget, second only to the National Microscopic Health Solutions Organization. The NMDD however, has been struggling in recent years. People around the world are getting fewer hours of sleep than ever, even with all the extra Oxygen Deprivation Specialists in the field. Between extra-large coffees, energy drinks, extra work hours and sleep-disruptive technology, their industry has been shrinking, along with their profits.

If you want to help a struggling economy, all you have to do is sleep. You'll be providing dozens of jobs, supporting dozens of families and, best of all, you'll be sleeping.

Every Day

When you fall asleep you die. But in the afterlife you get to choose a day of your life to re-live. In death the first thing you do is talk to the manager. He checks off the day you just lived from the master list and asks you to pick another. You go back and forth trying to figure out which days would be the best and how to live out your remaining ones. Since most people don't remember when they were babies, those days are usually the first to go. The next group is usually terrible days or the greatest days. It depends on the type of person and whether or not they want to get them out of the way or save them until the end.

The manager shows you the list of days left and each day has a few bullet points of the highlights and lowlights. There are a lot of days where nothing of note happened and there are no bullet points, so those are quick to come off the list. You've been saving the good days, but you finally pick a day when you were 16 where your high school crush talked to you for the first time. It was a good day, somewhere in the middle, and you're starting to long for some of the earlier, better memories.

The manager jots things down in his book and takes you away to the pod, where once inside, all your previous memories are wiped and you're transported back to that day you were a young sophomore. The manager sets it up so all of the days up to this one are in your memory bank, but you have no knowledge of anything that happens after, especially not about the manager. You live out your day and you're really happy when you pass your crush in the hall and have a brief conversation about English class. That conversation carries you through the afternoon and the rest of your classes and then you lie down in bed and hope that you dream about it. Once you drift off to sleep you come face to face with the manager again. The manager asks if you enjoyed it. You say that you did.

This goes on for all of the days that you lived. There are highs and lows and painful memories mixed with happy emotions. The rollercoaster ride is the same, but the hills tend to be more steep and prolonged. You re-live happy days after exciting days and sad ones after bad ones and hope to get them all over at once.

But there's one day that you don't even want to look at. There's one day on the manager's list that you can hardly bring yourself to think about. It's at the bottom of the list, the very last item, and before long it's the only one left. You stare at the manager and the manager stares back. No words are needed. All that's left between you and the day that you die is a clipboard and the manager, someone you don't really even know.

You start to tear up but hold them back from rolling down your face. You've known about this day since the beginning, it was mentioned in your first encounter with the manager, it just seemed like such a long time ago and you thought you had plenty of time. You start re-thinking your choices of days to live. Maybe you shouldn't have saved all the good days until the end, and then maybe this wouldn't be so hard. Or maybe you should have spread them out more and made everything feel longer and more powerful.

The manager looks up from the clipboard and asks if you're ready. You're still not sure, even after re-evaluating everything; you're not sure you can go back and die again. The manager tells you that you have no choice and that it's the only day left. Then the tears start streaking down your cheeks and you ask what happens when you die again.

"Will I come back here?" You ask.

"I can't tell you." The manager says. "That's not how it works."

Your mind starts reeling and you're filled with the wonderment of life after death all over again. You still can't stop crying and you wish things would have played out differently. If only you had done something different, you think. If only you had another chance.

Faced with an uncertainty and doubt of your choices, the manager walks you to the pod one last time.

HOW WE MET

I saw her in Canada. I was in Toronto. From across the street I saw her staring at me from a corner market that was selling magazines from around the world. She was in a bright yellow t-shirt tucked into denim capris. When our eyes met she looked back at her copy of a European art mag. I was mid-meal at a café but dropped my biscuit and started to walk across the busy traffic. A voice yelled my name. It was coming from behind me. I spun around to see a waiter following me, dodging cars and waving a bill in my direction. I hadn't paid and I guess that was frowned upon. I had never been to Canada before, I said. I didn't know any better. I reached for my pocket to hand over my credit card and looked back toward the magazine stand only to see the yellow shirt missing from the scene.

I saw her again in Brazil. I was on the beach, relaxing with a beer and she was out on the waves, surfing in a yellow-toned wetsuit just off in the distance. The waves were low and far between but I could tell she knew what she was doing. Her hair was wet and whipped over her shoulders as she turned her hips to catch the pulse of the wave. I was half-done with my bottle when she started paddling for shore. Soon enough she was in waist-high water and she tucked her board underneath her arm and walked closer yet. She finally saw me and stopped, turned around and headed back toward the endless water.

I saw her at a symphony. I was in row 50 and she was two ahead of me, but on the opposite side. She hadn't spotted me yet but I saw her as soon as the music began. Her eyes sparkled and her head nodded along to the beat. Every now and then she would smile at a precarious violin solo or tricky synch between beats. Her teeth were sparkling, her lips were red and her dress was a shimmering gold. She was everything I imagined she would be. During the intermission she didn't get up, so I didn't either. She turned and talked to the people around her, but their faces were a blur to me. All I could see was her smile, her perfect teeth, her perfect face. When intermission was over I didn't take my eyes off hers. When the music started again I didn't watch the symphony or the conductor or anyone else, I only watched this woman until the music stopped. I tried to find her afterwards but got caught in the midst of the overwhelming crowd of evening gowns and tuxedos.

I saw her again at the airport. She was on her laptop and taking notes on a legal pad, I was on my computer trying to waste time. She was at gate 43 and I was at 44. We were facing each other but there were at least 10 rows between us, all full of important, busy people eating meals, playing games, working on their laptops, reading books and sleeping. I saw her first again and looked up every minute to see if she had found me, tucked away in a corner, tethered to a pole with an outlet. She looked concerned, as if whatever was on her screen was the most important thing in the world. My screen was just solitaire. She bit her nails, picked her lips and tapped on the top of her screen. A voice came on from overhead. I didn't hear it, but she did. She packed her things and headed for her plane. She handed a little piece of paper to an airline worker and walked down the temporary hallway and out of my world once again.

I had seen her many times, but I never expected to see her here. I was at the store, buying bananas, trying to find some that weren't so green. I reached over for a perfect bunch of six when my hand bumped into another. I followed the hand to the arm to the elbow to the shoulder and stopped when I reached a face. I almost didn't believe it, but she was there, standing next to me at the bananas in the grocery store.

"Sorry," she said, as if we had never met before. Then I ran it through my mind and reminded myself that we, in fact, had never met before. I had seen her so many times in my dreams that I felt like she was a familiar friend. This woman of my dreams who I had never been able to explain before was here, pushing around a cart full of perishable goods.

"No, sorry, it's my fault." I said after regaining my sense of awareness. "I'm Dan, by the way."

"Stacy." She moved her hand away from the bananas and extended it to me. "It's nice to meet you."

"You have no idea."

EVERYBODY SLEEPS

The beauty about sleep is that everyone does it.

Some people sleep comfortably in a half-empty six-bedroom house, nestled tightly in their Egyptian-cotton luxury sheets. Some people sleep in a single bed, the only one in the house, with hand-me-down sheets with more moth holes than threads in their thread count.

Some people sleep in a hut, on a dirt floor covered in whatever they can find to keep them alive through the night. Others sleep in a three-bedroom family house, their spouse by their side, child in the room next door and dog cuddled in his own bed at the foot of theirs.

Some people sleep in a hospital bed with a total stranger next to them, separated only by a curtain and a social understanding. People come and go throughout the night and there are blinking lights and strange noises that keep them from getting more than two hours of sleep. Some people sleep on city streets with makeshift cardboard mats to lie on and thrown-out blankets and table covers from dumpsters to keep them above freezing.

Some people share a bed with their sibling because their mother can't afford anything else. They're cramped and squished in awkward poses but it's all they know so they get plenty of sleep. Other people sleep in a California king all by themselves, wondering why their marriage fell apart, hoping they can keep going on with their lives and worry themselves into an hour of sleep at best.

Some people sleep on a concrete floor, trapped in a place they don't want to be and wonder how to get out. They haven't showered in days, haven't eaten in almost nearly as many and pray to God every night that their situation gets better and they can go on to live. Others sleep soundly knowing that what they're doing is morally reprehensible but not worried because they don't have any morals anyway and they've never believed in God.

Some people sleep in a different bed every night, coming into the shelter just in time to grab one of the few beds that seem perpetually dirty. All night long the few belongings that they have are gripped tightly between their fingers for fear of someone else taking it while they sleep. Some other people sleep in a hyperbolic chamber, hoping that it will keep them young and refreshed as they grow old and start to worry about their longevity.

Some people sleep in tents underneath the canvas of the sky, feeling the ground beneath them and taking in the smell of the fresh air in the mountains. The fire they built a few feet from where they rest slowly fades and the noises of nature start to filter through the air. Some other people sleep in a hotel every evening. They're constantly on the run and the tray from their room-service meal sits on the end table, half eaten and on its way to the garbage. The TV flickers as the weary business traveler tries to get some sleep before the big presentation in the morning.

Some people sleep on the couch, having been kicked out of the bedroom by their significant other for some insignificant detail. It's not comfortable and they can only really sleep on their side, but they try to make the best out of the situation they're in. Other people sleep in their comfortable chair, physically unable to do anything about it. The nurses try to persuade them to move to their bed, but they somehow always end up on the chair, remote in hand, covered in a quilt.

Birds sleep in trees, fish sleep underwater. Elephants sleep standing up, possums sleep upside down. Flamingos sleep on one leg, cows sleep on all four. Hummingbirds sleep very little while bears sleep for an entire season.

Vampires sleep in coffins, mermaids sleep in castles underwater. Bigfoot sleeps in the forest and the Loch Ness monster sleeps in murky water. Leprechauns sleep in underground houses and abominable snowmen sleep in a cave to avoid the snow.

The beauty about sleep is that everyone does it. Whether adult or child, man or woman, real or imaginary, hooved animal or one with wings, all things everywhere must sleep, and while everyone and everything is busy sleeping, we're all vulnerable.

Waking Up

The instant you wake up your brain is unsure of itself once again. It tries to reconcile the differences between the past hours and now. Things in this world are more real and hard and familiar. The truth seems to be grounded in facts and objects are held down in images. People, faces, spaces and places are coming into focus and your brain is adjusting. It knows it needs to process different functions and trigger the workings of everyday life but it still can't help asking the question.

What just happened?